THE SATAN SNIPER'S MOTORCYCLE CLUB

BOOK 1

"When I was younger, I was a beggar by circumstance,
When I got older, I remained a beggar by choice."
Beggar

SHAN R.K

Cover by Shan R.K
Photographer: Shan R.K
Model: Ariya
Graphics: Shan R.K
www.shanrk.com

<u>Acknowledgment</u>:

A huge thank you to my husband. The continuous support you've shown me from the time I started this adventure is my courage in my darkest hour. You've always pushed me to be better, achieve greater. You are my biggest fan and my own personal hero.

For all those people who had
A rough start in life and never
Gave up!!!

For the full experience: -
Playlist:

1. The Chain Smokers ft Rozes – Roses
2. Dorothy – Raise hell
3. Dustin Lynch – Mind Reader
4. Brentley Gilbert – kick it in the sticks
5. The Civil Wars - Barton Hollow
6. Eli young band - Crazy girl
7. Gavin James – Bitter pill
8. Florida Georgia – Stay
9. Jake Owen - don't think I can't love you
10. John Newman – losing sleep

I

The wind is colder today, makes me wish I had something warmer than the thin hoody I nipped off some kid two years back. I shiver in the small space between the bins hearing the raucous coming from the building I'm leaning on.

A year ago, it was just a rundown 3-storey dump. From today, it'll be known as a club called, Lazers.

The people scream and cheer. Their loud laughs echo in my dead soul.

I've never known a day of being normal or having a hot plate of food to eat. I don't even know what it feels like to have a bath. The streets of Washington have been my home since the day I was born.

I think I stayed in the hospital a few times but I'm not sure, I was too young to remember.

It's safe to say my mother loved me a little too much, because she wouldn't give me up. She rather I be born without a blanket to keep me warm than abort me or give me up for adoption.

Many times, she explained things to me, she'd say that I was a love child, and my daddy would one day find us and take us to his home. But he never came, and my mother didn't seem too beat up about it either. As the years went on by, I learnt to survive on these streets, I even learnt to smile.

Somehow by sheer luck my mother managed to get me in a school when I turned seven.

I was the dirty kid.

The one with lice in her hair.

The pity child who was always taking the lunch or scraps other kids left on the back wall during break.

By the end of the first year they called me Street girl. No one played with me, but I never let their words or actions bother me.

I kept my eyes on my school work.

My mother told me that if I focused on my grades and finished school, I'd be able to get a job when I got older. I remember just thinking that, we wouldn't have to stay on these streets.

Shelters weren't an option; they were the worst place we could go. We once ended up in the one on 16th Street.

We both had nothing to eat for two days. We were starving and I was getting weak. There was no other choice.

My mother tried everything to get a buck but no one was feeling generous,

not even for some scraps to eat. It was during my summer break.

While most kids ate their bellies full in those weeks, I was lucky if I got one meal a day. I never had a full belly then, didn't even imagine what it could feel like, but I didn't complain. I was alive, had all my fingers and toes.

Whenever I did complain about hunger pangs or frozen fingers my mother said I could've been unluckier. I could've been born without my arms or legs.

My mother's sanity had been questionable from time to time but she never let me beg, even when I asked. She always stashed me in some corner behind a bin or in an alley. Sometimes on weekends I'd sit on the pavement watching the cars go by.

But the day we went to the shelter was a bad day. I'll never forget that day. The nip in the air sent chills in my body. My small feet tripping over itself trying to keep up with my mother's hurried steps.

Her grip on my hand was so tight, it pained.

We got there just as they were finishing up, and she rushed us straight to the queue for the free sandwiches. I think I was around eight.

A group of the people who ran the shelter saw me that day. They tried taking me away from my mother by locking me in some storage room. I was screaming and crying.

I remember how I bit the lady that pulled me away. I think I scratched her too, I'm not sure, it was a while ago.

Somehow my mother managed to get me out of there and we kicked down, and didn't stop until we were at the river. We sat in silence and ate a slice of the tuna sandwich she had with her.

She stole three sandwiches that day. I was old enough to know they always gave one per person. I wasn't sure how she managed that, but grateful, it kept us fed for three days.

It was the first and last time we ever sort out a shelter.

That was also the first time she warned me about the system. I remember her words,

"You listen to me kid. Those houses they'll put you in are far worse than living on the street. You can never get caught; you hear me."

I stared at her crazy green eyes, and knotted black hair, then I nodded. My mother's face was hollow, and her wrist so fragile, sometimes I feared she might just break and shatter into thousands of pieces. But she was tough and kept me safe.

She said bad things happened to the kids in the system. Many people thought she was crazy. Mad. But I believed her.

After that my mother always spoke to me about her life when she was younger, and the dangers she faced after entering a foster home.

At the ripe age of ten, I knew the horrors I'd face if I was taken away from her.

The rape and the abuse were what I dreaded the most. But I was born unlucky, because my mother got sick.

She was diagnosed with stage three lung cancer and didn't last two months after we found out.

I was just twelve when she died.

There were no parting touchy words she passed on to me.

No tears.

She just looked at me from the hospital bed.

And carried on looking even after the monitors blared through the room, even after the nurse lifted me up off the ground and carried a struggling me out of the room.

I could've maybe told myself that she smiled a little but I couldn't bring it to the forefront of my mind to have such foolish thoughts.

It was the same day, November 8th, that the system swallowed me in. I had no choice. Forced into it and for 2 weeks like any other 12-year-old faced with shit luck I stuck it out for a peanut butter sandwich in the morning and stale crackers at night.

But when your foster dad rapes you, you get the fuck out of dodge.

I did. But only after I took a tin opener to his throat.

I left the other kids in that shit hole and took my chances alone on the streets. I was bleeding and violated. My private places ached, but I didn't seek a hospital or anyone's help.

Instead I made my way to the train station that night and cleaned myself up in the public bathroom that smelled like shit and puke. But to me, it was just another day of surviving; just another day in this fucked up-ness we call life.

The tissue paper I used to wipe the evidence away as the tear leaked silently down my cheek, was the one thing I made sure of, to never let happen again.

9 years have passed since then. Not much has changed in my life. No magical happenings or great jobs.

I didn't even finish school.

I'm still living on Washington streets. Still begging for scraps, because no one wants to hire a homeless 21-year-old with no I.D. I tried, many, many times.

I even tried stripping; apparently you need a 'P H D' to do that too.

Only now the cold is making it fucking hard to even breathe. But nothing is making me come out of my spot in-between the dumpsters. This is like a fucking luxury hotel in my world. I could get a good 3 or 4 hours sleep here.

The owner of Lazers saw me around a few times, he said he wanted to talk to me tonight when the place closed. I only agreed because he offered me a hot meal, something I've never had before. And I'm sure I can take him if he tries anything. I haven't lived this long being nice.

To survive years on the streets, you need rules. The first one is never trust anyone. You do that and you'd have no one to identify your body. You'd be lucky it even made it to the morgue. Or worse, you could end up sold as a fucking prostitute for small pocket change. There's no way out of that one. Those pimps get you hooked on any crap they feel like sticking up your veins and it isn't always drugs.

The second rule- if you're a female, always stink, even if you manage to get to the river or a tap. You never clean up too nicely. Smelling bad keeps fuckers away.

The third rule- don't think someone is your friend, there's no fucking friends in this place, everybody wants something. I made that mistake a few times and almost got shot by a street gang last year, when this girl Tally told them I stole her drugs, the same drugs she shot up her veins.

And the fourth, and this is an important one, never steal. Many of us do, well most. I did it one time, just once, to a kid 2 years ago. I was fucking cold and hadn't eaten for days. I saw him stash a ten in the front pocket of his hoody and thought fuck it. I got the hoody, but only after he beat the fuck out of me. It turned out he was only short and was actually 17.

After he beat me, he took pity on me and gave me a hundred, it was sick, but I took the cash and it kept me fed for months. Since then, I hadn't had any problems. No run ins with trouble, well at least not anything worth adding to my nightmares. I never said I'm innocent.

You'd think I went through hell to survive on the street. Truth is, us homeless folks are all trying to survive. We spend more time fighting against nature and saving our strength until our next meal than we do fighting each other. Not to say that I have a clean slate or it's all peachy.

The back door next to the red dumpsters I'm resting between bangs open,

"I'm fine Zero!" A sweet female voice says.

"Den and Spades with us," Her heels click so close to me. I still.

"I didn't want you to worry. I wanted to come." There's a pause, no footsteps.

"You know I will." Her voice softens.

I roll my eyes, it's obviously a guy.

I liked a boy once, blue eyes, red Curly hair. He worked by the supermarket down town, he was cute, around my age now. I think I was fourteen or fifteen.

I used to beg three blocks away from the supermarket and instead of saving for a loaf of bread, the moment I had enough cash I went to the store to buy a lollipop. This happened on average- twice a day.

I'd wash my face and tidy myself up before I got there and I'd smile. I hated smiling, but he was cute.

The first few times I went, he scowled, looking at me like I'm gonna steal, as if.

About a week later a sign was posted on the display window, 'no homeless folks allowed'.

I didn't think it meant me, I made sure to clean up before I entered the place. I didn't have my always stink rule at that time, so I didn't think I looked homeless.

So, I was surprised when a few steps into the supermarket, he came storming up to me with a security guy trailing behind him screaming,

"Didn't you see the sign. No beggars, get your dirty ass outa here."

People stopped and watched but nobody said anything. I never liked a boy again, in fact when I see them, I look the other way except one time. One other time I liked a man. One other time I thought I loved him with all my heart. One other time and it was the last.

This girl is obviously lucky; I bet she's dating some guy in one of those fancy suits. I can't see her face, but just hearing her voice, I can tell she's a softy that wouldn't survive an hour in my world.

She's still talking to the person on the phone, but I can't hear much anymore because she's moved further away from me. I shift into my corner, my body still covered by a cardboard box I found in the dumpster. It's a few minutes later that I hear her heels drumming closer to the club, closer to me. She's going really fast now by the way her heels are clicking on the tar. Maybe she's upset. I listen quietly because I ain't got nothing better to do, it's not like I have a TV or radio.

What's that sound? Other people's feet, heavy footsteps. My heart begins to race as I recognize those heavy footfalls, it's a man, shit, not man, men.

Scream bitch, scream for help, but she doesn't.

She's going to get herself in some deep trouble now. There's a struggle. I can hear a muttered curse and the sound of her shoe dropping,

"I'm a Satan Sniper you fuckwad, let me go." Her screech sounds like she's struggling. They must have her against a wall, or in a strong hold, shit.

I don't see anything, only hear one of the men's response,

"I don't give a fuck. After I'm done with you bitch my friend here is gonna fuck you until you bleed and then I'm gonna slit your fucking throat."

I listen to the swearing and her weak wails. Shit, she's going to get raped. Should I help? I wanna scream for her but what if they have friends around the alley just keeping watch, damn it to hell.

With a pounding heart I remove the cardboard box off my body. Once I'm sure they can't hear me, I crawl slowly out of my nest. They don't notice me, but I ain't surprised by this. I give it a good few seconds then I peep around the dumpster.

The one guy is African American, bald and meaty. He's holding her neck in a chokehold with a gun pointed to her head.

The blonde guy is trying to get her jeans down, and struggling. Her make up is running down her cheeks, red locks sticking up in all directions.

God, she's so tiny and short.

I creep closer, sure not to draw attention to myself.

Blondie finally gets pissed when her jeans don't come down and slits it open, with a knife.

Wrong move.

Her spiked heel of her right boot gets him first in the nuts, then in the face when he bends down. She does some twisty move and gets out of the other guys neck hold. The men make a quick recover and both start hitting her.

Blondie slaps her across the face as the other guy upper cuts her. She screams and bends down, weaving.

Fuck, I know that if I don't help, they gonna kill her. I creep closer, still keeping to the dark. Her elbow makes contact with the throat of the man holding the gun, cutting off his oxygen.

The girl got moves.

His hands instinctively go for his neck causing him to drop the weapon a few feet away from me.

I don't think, just act.

Running out of the shadows I sprint to the gun, pick it up, click the safety off, and pull the trigger.

First bullet to the African Americans head, then to the blonde fucker's heart. Both kill shots, both drop dead.

How I managed to do that, is another story I don't wanna remember, my nightmare. The reason why I still beg on the streets for scraps. Why I never finished school, why I can't even get a fucking ID.

And why the world would always just know me as *Beggar*.

II

I speed up the incline at seventy miles per hour, my bike is killing it. The smell of burning rubber is doing no justice to the actual heat my Harley's taking. If the cops flashed me now, I'd be fucked. Not only did I leave my license back at the room we're staying in, but the club has no jurisdiction in DC.

The old deputy, Willis was shot a few weeks back. Although the bullet grazed him, he took his family up North for some desk job. The Prez didn't wanna bust the man's balls. We don't even have a chapter this side and hardly spend time in DC to really care enough to bribe him to stay.

The women wouldn't stop nagging about seeing the new club that opened up tonight which is the only reason we're here now.

I was in no way driving 23 hours so they could dance in some club because some punk ass Rockstar was attending.

My first vote was no but Chadley talked my woman, Falon into going.

I waited for her to say something, but she didn't.

One of the new prospects, Den brought it up the next day after church. He publicly announced Falon was joining the girls. I was fucking angry. She didn't say shit when I asked about it again the same night.

I understood that she wanted to keep us quiet because her dad was the President. The man and I served two tours together.

But keeping stuff from me was not something I was going to take, which was why I decided to say fuck-it to all her plans and tell the guys. The sooner I claimed her ass the better my life would be.

When I showed up the morning, they were due to leave, I could tell Falon was surprised. I waited to see if she would get on another brother's bike so I could disfigure the fuckers face. But one thing about Falon, she knows when not to push her luck.

She jumped behind me without a second thought. I was thrilled, but still too pissed. Which is why when we got to the hotel, I didn't book a room for myself. I doubled with Storm, our VP.

Unlike my other brothers, Storm knows about Falon and I. He doesn't like keeping it quiet, and always gives me shit when we're alone. Neither the fuck do I, but I do it for Falon, surprisingly Storm is doing it for me.

Falon is a petite 26-year-old, with a few heartbreaks, nothing too serious from what she's let slip.

I'm a 31-year-old man with a fakuva lot of baggage. But I didn't want her at the back of another brother's bike, so angry or not, here I was.

It didn't mean that we were okay. Right now, however, I wish we were.

I turn into 18th Street and my stomach tightens with a sick feeling. If I don't get to Lazers in the next few minutes my woman is not going to be okay, call it a hunch or 8 years serving my country, but I'm never wrong.

When Falon whispered, "someone's coming" and cut the call. I got on my bike and drove.

No helmet or jacket. I didn't tell the brothers nothing, but knowing Storm he'll figure somethings going down.

He ain't the Vice President of The Satan Sniper's Motorcycle Club for nothing.

3 weeks, 21 days I have been doing this running around shit with Falon and I hate it. Keeping secrets from my brothers, making Storm do it too, it ain't right. I'm the Enforcer of the club. My dad was one of the 6 original members that started the MC nearly 40 years ago.

When I told Falon I wanted her in my bed every night, she gave me a blow job and offered to fuck me bare. She was that happy, then no show for two weeks. I had to hunt her down at her ma's house in Barfa.

First she acted like it was nothing and she was just busy, which had me walking back to my bike.

It was a few days later when she came looking for me at the Clubhouse, eyes all puffy and shit, telling me she didn't want to stress her dad, and that we should wait six months to tell him.

My first reaction was hell no, but a week later I said fuck it, I missed her.

We spoke it out, more like banged it out and agreed to give things 3 months. I knew the real reason was that she wanted to be sure. I'm not a sure thing for her and I don't blame Falon for having doubts.

Truth is, I have them too, but Falon is the closest thing I'd ever gotten close to loving.

Like most of my brothers that make up The Satan Snipers, I was conditioned not to feel emotion, not to feel remorse.

When we joined the special ops program 8 years ago, we didn't think we'll ever be free from it all. But Falon had a way of making one forget. No way was I going to let one of the other brothers have her.

Falon has known this life since she was born. She never let it harden her though. Her dad Rounder was 15 when he found out his ex-girlfriend Molly was pregnant with Falon. His dad was the sergeant-at-arms of The Satan Snipers at the time.

At sixteen while my blood brother, Thorn was fucking anything with a cunt, Rounder was a single parent changing his 3-month-old daughter's diapers.

Apparently, Molly just upped and left.

With the help of the club and Rounder's mother Haze, Falon turned out pretty good.

I stop my bike outside Lazers. The smell of alcohol, cigarettes and cheap perfume pollute the air in high quantities.

The rave music coming from Lazers is outweighing the other nightclubs. A crowd waiting to join in on the fun that's coming from inside is so long, there's no way I'll be able to bargain my way in. But right now, I don't give a fuck.

Normally I wouldn't draw attention to myself, it's my nature to blend in. I was trained to be a ghost and shadow in the army's special ops, and this is going against everything I've been taught, but I need to go fetch my woman.

I jump off my bike and head to the front door. The bouncer is clueless as I walk right up to him. He's too busy flirting with the tall willowy girl with the blonde hair and fake tits.

Two consecutive shots choose that moment to shock everyone. It's coming from behind the club. I'm already rounding the corner in a run. The sound of sobbing speeds my movement. I pause in my tracks doing a double take at the scene before me.

Falon is in a hunched position. Her jeans are torn off, laying in pieces beside her as she shakes with uncontrolled sobs. I give her body a quick scan. Besides the torn jeans she's intact.

I can't afford to process anything beyond basic survival right now, not with the tall hooded figure holding a gun and two men dead on the floor.

I edge closer to the figures back.

I'm unnoticed.

My moves silent and breathing evened out.

"Hey Girl, you okay?" The voice is dry, rough and hoarse from lack of water or not talking. I don't care but it's definitely female.

Falon lifts her head toward the female. Her face smeared with make up running down her cheeks. I fight the need to show her any compassion or make sure she acknowledges me. I got to stay focused.

"Ththth...anks," Falon stutters, hiccupping.

The hooded female lowers the gun to her side and I go in.

Gripping her arms to the side I pull the gun out from between her hands. She's fighting me but quickly loses spirit when I release her.

So, she doesn't like to be touched, interesting and opposite to Falon, who craves affection.

Not wasting time, I empty the gun, all the while noticing this girl's breathing is labored.

Ignoring the two opposite women, I jog across to the dead men, rubbing our prints off the gun, and put the two dead men prints on it. I finish with the blonde guys cold hand and lay the gun next to him as the back-door swings open.

People swarm through as my gaze goes to where Falon is, but she's not there. At my full height I scan the crowd and see the hooded girl pulling Falon in-between the dumpster. The hood girl is quick and doesn't understand what the fuck she just did, who she just saved.

Not only did she save the Prez daughter's life, but she saved my woman's pride too.

The people crowd the dead bodies, some taking pics, others screaming or crying. Majority are just standing there staring at the two dead guys, and wondering what the fuck happened.

Wisp rushes over to me, her hazel eyes glassy, lips thinned. Her short denim skirt barely covers her pussy. The busty leather thing she has covering her tits is no better.

Storm and Texas are going to turn her hide.

We might be an all sexist club but the guys who have claimed one of our own, whether temporarily or permanent take their commitments very fucking seriously.

And there's no doubt that Texas isn't going to let her slide this one out with a few fucks. We don't mind the girls dressing in skimpy shit around the Clubhouse. In public we mind, we're territorial motherfuckers and have killed for much less.

The women know better. Wisp knows better.

I kiss her head so I don't draw attention to us.

"Call Den and Spade, and make sure you give a heads up to Storm, cops are gonna be here any minute."

I retreat backwards, my steps are slow as not to make things obvious. Stopping next to the dumpster, I lean on it casually.

"Falon, we need to go baby the cops are gonna be here any minute."

"We take the girl."

It takes me a second to realize that was an order, shit, this bitch really saved my woman to have her standing up to me.

Falon might keep secrets and try to be tough, but it's her nature to be pliant.

She's never given an order, but right now she's speaking to me as the President's daughter, not as her man.

What she doesn't know is, in no fucking way was I leaving the hooded chick behind. When she killed those guys, she passed the biggest test of The Satan Snipers, we have to protect her and take her in.

But I'm a fucking man, if my woman wants to think it was her choice and she's calling the shots then that's what she gets.

"Ok, let's move."

They both start to come out, the other girl still covered in a hoody comes first and fuck, what's that smell.

I sniff closer to her, she reeks, yuck.

I retreat a few steps away from her when Falon comes out wearing haggard ripped jeans that are a few sizes too big.

At least she's covered. It's then, it clicks. This girl is homeless, she was sleeping here. I grab hold of Falon's arm rubbing my thumb on it for only a second. It's not in me to show too much affection unless I'm fucking, but the small show of affection lets her know I was worried.

We start walking, the other girl following behind Falon, until we stop where I parked my bike. The cops are already stationed, ushering people out of the way, so they can close the doors. No one gets in or out.

I pull the girls to my bike, hearing the roars of my brother's bikes coming up the road.

The three of us wait for them.

Storm turns his black chrome and parks it directly in the middle of all the chaos whilst the others stay on their bikes and park across the street.

He pulls his helmet off and I notice his cut missing.

A quick look across the road, I know the others are also missing their cuts. They were obviously warned in time and decided not to draw the unwanted attention.

The faded jeans and white t-shirt I'm wearing makes me blend in too.

I watch Storm ruffle his brown hair until it's all pushed back. His eyes scan the bustling crowd, until it lands on us.

I got Falon's hand in a tight grip, and she's holding the homeless girl's arm. So, she doesn't like men touching her, I wonder how fucked up this homeless girl is.

Storm is a few inches taller than my 6ft 4in, but suffered a back injury a few years back. The hunch he has now is telling me that my brother's back is killing him, shit.

"We gotta leave now," He says.

"Prez called, he spoke to the detective, they giving us ten to get moving."

I look Falon over, her skin isn't glowing, it's green instead and we don't have a fucking cage to put her in. She's gonna have to hold it in a bit longer.

Storm sees my hesitation and notices the hooded girl.

His interest in her makes me want to barf. He hasn't smelt the bitch yet. I would smile if we had more time or if the circumstances were different.

"She can ride with you, Falon's with me."

He doesn't argue, he walks to his bike and the homeless girl follows.

I don't hear what she tells him or he tells her, but the smile playing on his lips when she says something almost makes me want to punch it off his face.

Fuck, What the hell is wrong with me?

Falon and I cross the street just as Jade, Wisp, Chadley, Den, Spade and Venus run up to us.

"I'm so sorry Fal," Den says

My jaw tightens, "You not yet. But when I'm fuckin' done with you, you would be motherfucker."

Falon touches my arm, it's the first contact she's voluntarily given me since I found her hunched over.

"Please, Zero not now."

My death glare trained on him makes my message clear, I'm dropping this now, but we far from fucking done, he messed up and big time.

Den had one task: - watch Falon.

Spade was looking after the other girls, more so Wisp and Chadley, who couldn't protect themselves.

Den should've paid more attention, did what he was fucking told to do.

We cross the road and the others do well to be quiet, especially 'cause I know the girls are dying to ask what happened.

When Texas, Knight and Bull are in hearing shot, still on their bikes I order them,

"We shoot straight to Kanla, two stops. We need to get to church." The lot nods. Knight's face, grim, because he knows what that means.

Wisp glances across the road watching Storm. Curious I follow her lead.

What the fuck, Storm is slipping his helmet on the homeless girl's head, not the spare one he keeps for Wisp.

Her hoody is down and it's darker where they're standing at the edge of the pavement.

Storm leans on his bike and the light to the club goes on.

My eyes glue to the vision that's all away across the road.

Her skin is so fucking pale and hair so dark.

I don't stop watching them until her helmet is fully on her head and her face now hidden behind the dark glass.

Slowly her hand lifts to rest on Storm's shoulder. I feel something, but I'm not sure what the hell I'm feeling and I don't fucking like it.

The small huff from Wisp is noticed by all of us and pulls me from the fucking trance.

She's pissed off that he's giving his helmet up for the homeless girl, but Wisp doesn't know what she did for Falon. And we don't have time to talk and explain shit.

I grab Falon by the arm. She hasn't said a word to anyone. I move across the road just as the other brothers rev their bikes getting ready to hit the road.

By the time we're getting on my bike, Storm has the homeless girl's arms wrapped around him, and his speeding off to take his place in the front next to Bull, our road captain.

"Hang in there Baby."

"I'm fine, let's just get out of here." Falon's abruptness doesn't sound good.

I know I should comfort her but we gotta move. We can't deal with this now.

If I show Falon a shred of comfort she's going to break. It's all over her face.

Once her arms are secured around my waist, my bike throttles and we're gone.

It's two minutes when I take my place at the back of the formation, at the back of my brothers.

Watching them, protecting them, guarding them. It's why I am the enforcer of The Satan Sniper's Motorcycle Club. I've always had this way of seeing when shit is about to happen.

We hit the freeway and I catch a glimpse of my VP with the girl on his back, and I just know things are about to get complicated.

III

The wind is blowing through my hair, the guy whose name is Storm, is driving like this is his last ride, and I love it. I'm glad I didn't chicken out, and gladder that I'm going to have a hot bath and hot meal when we arrive at this Clubhouse, he told me about.

He said I'm one of them now. Storm said that I'll never have to be hungry again. It's crazy that I agreed, but his brown kind eyes told me he was certain, that he'll take care of me and I believe him.

For the first time I believe someone besides my mother and It's stupid I know. But somehow, I feel lighter. I've never felt lighter, ever.

I didn't get to see Falon's boyfriend nicely, but the guy is tall and imposing. I'm scared of him. When his gaze tracked me from across the road at Lazers I just wanted to wither under his scrutiny.

He probably thought I didn't notice but I did.

I watched him from the corner of my eyes as he stood across the road surrounded by his people.

He was staring at me, and it made me feel like he was a hunter and I, his prey.

Doesn't he know that prey never wants to get caught?

But Storm has a warmth that I choose to trust. I saw interest spark in his gaze, it wasn't sexual but more curiosity and then understanding, when I asked,

"Do I have to hold you and shit?"

I Inked that down to a good thing. He didn't mask his face, he didn't look down on me, but showed me that he understood. And I knew I'd be safe with him.

Truth is, I was hungry and cold, so fucking cold. After I saved the girl, and her boyfriend swiped the gun, something told me that I was going to have to go with these people, even if Falon hadn't insisted.

There was no way her boyfriend was leaving me. I was going willing or not. I had a choice to make, I could go willingly and get treated well or I could go by force, and they'll spit on me and treat me like crap.

I chose the logical route, willingly, and I'm glad, especially since this guy named Storm is taking me on a ride of my life.

We stop at a gas station, about sixty miles away from Washington D.C. The bikes all park in one of the four gas lines. My arms are still snug around Storm's waist, my legs shaky and itchy.

I can just imagine what people in cars must be thinking seeing all these big machines moving together. I wonder if it keeps them up at night?

The lights in the garage are bright, even with the helmet on.

I've never been out at night, normally I'm out cold by now, or somewhere hidden. There's this weird feeling to it, I can't even explain it.

These bikers are obviously naturals to the call of the night.

I watch Falon and her boyfriend climb off his motorcycle together and head for the garage shop hand in hand.

My stomach grumbles at the thought of what they going to buy, reminding me I haven't eaten since this morning.

I lost out on that hot meal now.

Guess I'm just going to have to stick it out until I get to this Clubhouse.

After our tank is filled, Storm taps my thigh causing me to jerk, and my heart rate to spike.

I don't like it when men touch me.

I don't like it when they touch my thighs especially.

I want to run.

My instincts are telling me to jump off, but my brain is telling me stay, they aren't a danger to me. There are too many witnesses for Storm to do anything. I start shaking and Storm immediately gets off the motorcycle.

My body starts to shiver, vision darkening.

I focus on his helmet coming off his head. I watch his stubble jaw and thick brows covering his light brown gaze.

There's a twinkle that is close to a smile tugging his lips as his eyes dance in humor.

"I don't like to be touched." I croak pulling the helmet off.

As force of habit, I slip my hood over my head.

It's going to be a hard habit to break when I get to their Clubhouse. Let's hope they don't mind it too much.

He watches me while I slip my hair under my hood.

"Ok, no touching, got it, you want a bite?"

"Yes, something cold. I'm waiting for that hot meal you promised me." *It's true.*

He bursts out laughing, and I can feel the change in atmosphere.

Years on the street teaches you something that no amount of training ever will, A sixth sense.

When we parked, the other bikers were easy and calm, now the tension is thick in the air, and all the biker's eyes are on us.

I drop my head, Storm notices it and he turns his back to me.

I look up and instantly catch Falon's boyfriend watching me.

Storm walks a few steps, then spins around opening his arms,

"Well? You wanna eat or what?"

I swivel my head to face him fully. A small smile paints my lips realizing he's talking to me, and quickly I run after him,

"I never say no to food!"

He laughs again as we enter the garage shop with Falon and her boyfriend in tow.

I don't stare at either of them, even though with my hood covering most of my face I could and they wouldn't even know.

Storm gets a basket,

"Help yourself girl."

I smile under my hoody, and start putting chips and two sandwiches in the basket, mindful that I shouldn't push my luck.

I snap a can of coke from the shelf. My hand on a second for Storm.

"What's your name?" Someone asks me and that voice makes my pulse speed up, and freezes me in place.

He's talking to me, it's not Storm, it's the *boyfriend*.

I don't know what to say, how to answer without lying.

If there's one thing I like to do, it's lie. I'm a good one too.

I know they wouldn't believe what I say but I got to buy myself time and say something.

They'll let me go if they trust me, and if I'm lucky I could get a few nights of sleep at their Clubhouse maybe even a job or some shit.

I did save that girl's life. And a fresh start is something I needed for a long time.

"What's yours?" My question is meant to get him to shut it.

He surprises me at how quickly he answers,

"Zero, now your turn."

I glance at Storm and put the coke in the cart. He sees my shaking hands and sends a death glare to Zero, who hasn't looked away from me.

It unnerves me, the heat of his stare blistering, still I won't face him.

I don't want to.

I don't want to put a face to the guy who has me riddled in fear.

"Don't you have a name, something?"

Why won't he drop it?

Just leave it alone, I want to scream at him.

Why is he trying to get a reaction out of me?!

Why must he look at me like that? I can feel it. I don't need to see him.

I want to hide behind Storm, even though I barely know the man.

The biker's insistence is tempting me to tell him something mean and hurtful but I bite my tongue.

Instead I put one of the pudding things I see on top of the sandwich shelf into his basket, mindful that it's four dollars and walk the two steps to stand next to Storm.

I sneak a glance at Storm who is quiet and sending very hateful glances to his supposed to be brother.

Zero doesn't move away, he's not liking my silence.

It's only after a tense minute that he seems to listen to Storm's unspoken words and drops it by flying past us.

Falon is behind him, and gives me a sad smile before she follows the guy who I still haven't looked at.

"If you don't want any more of that." Storm tilts his head to the couple, "I suggest you figure out a name for yourself before we get to Kanla. We about eighteen hours away. We should get there about nine tomorrow evening, we'll stop in the next four hours or so for the night."

"Where about is that?"

"Eighty miles out Houston."

I dry whisper, "I'm going to Texas."

His eyes sparkle when he starts filling the basket with more sandwiches and cans.

"Yeah, Kanla isn't well known. We moved from Houston to Kanla, 3 years back. The town was getting run down by a gang of drug dealers. We brought them down and took the turf for our own. The plan was to go back to Houston but the town was so welcome and shit. And we needed a place to stay that wasn't so central and gave us proper privacy. With a population of around 2 thousand, Kanla seemed perfect. The 9 of us left Houston and started our own Chapter in Kanla. You gonna love the place. You gotta meet Rounder and Killer when we get there first though, but after that I'll introduce you properly to the others."

I walk on in front of him when he quietens, not sure what to say to that.

These bikers are clearly dangerous but Storm is growing on me.

No one has ever spoken to me so much besides my mother, and she's dead now.

I'm anxious to get to Kanla, more so than them. I can't wait to get that bath.

Gosh, I wonder how hot the water is going to be?!

And the food, are they going to cook meat?

My mouth waters, and for the next 10 minutes or so, I'm in my own little world.

I don't let it bother me when the lady standing behind Storm and I, moves a few steps away from me, I know I smell.

And I don't let it bother me when the male cashier sends me a reproachful look.

I'm too busy in my own world, my mind firmly on what my first hot meal is going to be.

IV

I'm barely keeping it together. I know I should let it rest, but I can't drop it.

I need to know her name.

I don't know why, but my gut is riding me hard on this.

My instincts are telling me it's important. Storm stood up to me in the garage giving me no other option but to drop it.

When Falon and I walked away from them, she gave me shit about not frightening the girl off too. But whether they agree or not I'm going to get my answer.

We park outside the Inn, 6 hours out of DC. We are well past ready to go down for the night.

Falon is huddled on a bench, talking with Jade, Chadley and Venus. Storm is talking to his new bff, and I don't like it.

I'm the Enforcer. If there's even a thread that she's a danger to my club I need to know.

How the fuck am I supposed to do that if my VP keeps giving me fucking warning glares?

Wisp marches over to them, her short form making up the distance fast. She's changed into a jean but still has that bust contraption she calls a t-shirt on.

Texas moves in slow, keeping a few steps behind her with an unlit cigarette dangling from his lips.

I move closer to them.

Maintaining a wide gap, as not to alert Wisp to my presence. There's no way I'm staying hidden from Storm when he keeps shooting me warning glances from across the lot.

Wisp goes to stand forcefully between Storm and the homeless girl, screaming,

"Is it not enough that she gets your helmet and rides on your back. You also gotta ignore me now." She shoves his chest when he keeps quiet.

He doesn't move, just crosses his arms over his chest and tilts his head down.

Texas moves naturally to stop her, but I signal him to stay put with a shake of my head.

This is long overdue.

"Planning on spending the night with her while you at it, ha? Well let's forget about Wisp for a second. Oh wait, let's forget about her for the night 'cause she is just a bed warmer. I am so done with your shit Storm. I know about your trips to Liston Hills and I'm done."

Everyone is quiet, waiting for the other shoe to drop. The homeless girl drops it, when she pulls down the hood, and my cock beats to come out behind my zipper.

And ain't I just the motherfucker of good timing.

I walk towards them, mindful of my hard-on happening behind my denims as her face becomes clearer.

Still watching the scene play out but not comfortable standing so far, I stop only 3 feet away.

The others are also staring, but forming a circle to surround them. We might want to watch things play out but it doesn't mean we want extra eyes and ears on our people.

The girl is pale, her eyes are black, pitch fucking black and so big under thick eyebrows.

She has a dirt mark staining her cheek and It takes every bit of self-control not to walk up to her and wipe it off.

I swallow, hard, and as if she hears it, she turns to face me. Everything fades away, all my brothers, all the girls besides her.

Her eyes tell me so much. They are the eyes of a person haunted, a girl who has seen things that no girl her age should see.

A protectiveness I've felt only for certain people shrouds me as I watch this girl, who is a puzzle I am yet to perfectly fit in place.

She breaks our connection and looks at Wisp's short form. I take time to profile her. She's around Falon's age, but life on the streets could've aged her, especially going from her voice. She's been there a while so she could be younger, much younger. She's thin and very tall, like 5ft 9in.

The same raspy sound I think of, says,

"You his girl?"

Wisp and Storm are too busy staring daggers at each other to pay the girl any heed.

"Lady, you Storm's woman?" she says louder, making me harder and I'm sure some of my other brothers too. Fuck, who talks like that. Her voice is hypnotic.

Wisp spins around, all her attention now focused on the homeless girl, shit, I hate calling her that. I wish she'll give us a name.

"I was, now he's free," Wisp practically spits in the girl's face.

Then Wisp does something bad, she sticks her nose higher and takes a step closer to the homeless girl, sniffing her,

"And have a fucking bath, you reek like dogs' shit." Wisp pushes past Storm who doesn't seem to care about her. antics.

He has been done with her for some time, she just wasn't getting the memo.

I expect Wisp to go straight for the girls but she surprises me by going back to Texas who instantly starts walking her away.

I follow behind them so I can get Falon, who is huddled up between Venus and Chadley, all the while ignoring my traitorous dick.

"I do stink. It's not safe on the streets if I'm clean."

Those words pause me in my track, she says it loud so we all hear her. I've never heard a female's voice so raspy before.

Soon after she speaks, Knight and Storm are laughing at her confession, no doubt trying to lighten the mood and hopefully save the poor girl some embarrassment.

I don't look back even though I want to. I head straight for Falon, her blue eyes lost when she sees me and I know I've fucked up.

I've been worried about another mysterious woman without a fucking name. Getting my dick hard for a pretty face, when the woman I plan to claim as my own and have a future with was almost raped.

Shit, I fucked up big time and I know I got to fix it.

I touch Falon's face with my fingers, her gaze softening under my touch. Venus and Chadley move out of the way, and I swoop Falon up, ignoring the gasp of the two girls seated down, and the eyes of my brothers.

She cuddles her face in the crook of my neck, and I don't let her go for twenty minutes.

It's how long it takes us to get our room sorted out.

Falon is out by the time we get to the room.

I lay her on the bed, and start stripping off her boots. She stirs when I get to the jeans but doesn't wake.

I pull up her t-shirt, revealing the purple and blue bruises forming on her stomach and ribs. Her small pouch of flesh on her abdomen she always complains about is now red with finger marks.

I graze the pads of my fingers gently across the bruises, all the while watching her features under the dim glow of the side lamp.

She's relaxed, and sleeping, but I'm anything but.

That homeless girl saved my woman. I want to hate her for stirring up things in me, for making me want to protect her when I have no business feeling that way about a woman I just met, especially when I got sweet Falon with me. I can't.

Falon is my future, she's real. I know who she is. I've known her most of her life. Falon's perfect.

What I'm feeling for that homeless girl is totally normal, I'm the Enforcer, and technically unofficially she's already one of us.

I'm supposed to feel protective around her.

Who wouldn't? A young girl living on the streets.

And my dick getting hard, well that's understandable, I haven't had sex in three days.

With Falon denying me the right to claim her and keeping stuff away from me I just wasn't feeling it.

I shake Falon's shoulder.

"Baby, you need to get up." She stirs but doesn't wake.

"Falon, come on," I try again, "We need to talk."

She mumbles something but after a few minutes opens those blue depths I have come to know so intimately.

Her face is all puffy and shit, her red hair sticking up all over the place. I swipe my index finger across her lips.

She gives me a small smile,

"Are you going to tell me you told me so?"

My gaze softens, "No baby, I'm just fucking relieved that you alive, but I need to know what happened."

She sits still watching my hand rub her thigh. Falon once told me it calms her when I do it.

"Ah," she sighs.

"We were talking on the phone. I wasn't really paying attention to where I was, and I walked further away. I ended up on the other side, but by then the two guys leaning against the wall saw me. I told you someone's coming and cut the call, then walked to the club doors. I wasn't sure if they were following me."

Her voice hitches, "I..I started going faster and I would've made it."

She sniffs, still not meeting my eyes.

"but my heel got stuck and I lost balance for a second, and then they grabbed me."

Her tortured eyes finally lift up, "The girl came."

I watch the half-truth come before it leaves her lips in a rush,

"She grabbed the guys gun and shot them. You know the rest."

"Did they rape you?"

"No." She turns away from my comforting hand and sobs into the pillow. I'm at a complete loss.

I lift my woman up, and she instantly nestles in my arms.

"I'm so sorry baby."

She cries harder.

She practically crawls onto me until her body is wrapped tightly around mine.

I've always liked Falon's shortness.

People always stare when we're together in public. She's barely 5 ft 3in like her mama and tiny, apart for her rack.

The sex is great.

She's mostly on top because I fear crushing her, and we never take it slow which I like.

All in all, the woman is a good woman.

She's a great cook, good in the bedroom, knows how to act and dress.

Plus, she's faithful.

And I'm sure she put up a fight with those assholes who tried to rape her. I rub her back in circles, hushing words in her hair.

I never told Falon I love her, I know she needs the words. I should say it. She's told me many times, but I can't.

I feel deep emotions for her, care about her, but even now that I got her in my lap, vulnerable and bruised after such a fucked-up night, I can't say the words.

I feel sorry for her, angry that those motherfuckers hurt my woman, but I don't feel that undying need for vengeance, that increase in emotion that my woman could've got hurt.

I tell myself it's because the men are dead, because there's no revenge to be dealt. Truth is I think I'm just incapable of love. I'm incapable of that emotion.

A half 'n hour passes before she's asleep in my lap. I put her into the bed and leave the room to give her space and go to the one place I know I'm going to get the answers I seek.

V

I'm in a hotel room and I just had a hot shower. It's AMAZING.

Christmas and New Year might have come 21 years too late, but it sure as hell came early this year.

My two weeks in the system didn't mean I had a hot shower. I had a warm one a few times. Being the new kid meant I had to shower last and by then the water was bordering on Luke warm on a good day.

And cold most of the other times.

Today I got the shower first and the stinging of the water on my back and hair was sensational.

I scrubbed myself with the bar of soap over and over again. I used all the shampoo on my hair, getting as much knots out as I could.

When I got out of the shower my skin was shriveled up. The steam was everywhere, even on the mirror.

I laughed, and it felt good.

Storm knocked on the door asking what was so funny, my answer was,

"I could get use to this."

He was quiet for a good few moments, then he banged on the door.

"Hurry your ass up in there, I gotta take a leak."

Now, my hair is dripping on the floor while I'm rummaging through Storm's bag for a t-shirt, mindful of the condoms I keep touching.

Storm just slipped in the bathroom we're sharing. He got us a double room, with two single beds.

After his girlfriend dumped him, the two of us took a slow walk to our room. He told me that Wisps 'temper tantrum' was bound to happen.

Apparently Wisp and him weren't actually dating, Texas and him were sharing her.

But he still spent time talking about the reason for Wisp's behavior, A girl named, Kylie Bray.

She's related to one of the brothers, the guys sister.

Storm met her a few months back and only recently she agreed to go on a date with him.

Storm showed me pictures of Kylie from his phone. She's the perfect image of rich and privileged. Her skin and teeth is all flawless with a smile so big you swear she's a celebrity without needing any confirmation.

When I voiced my opinion, Storm told me she was anything but and he'll introduce me to her.

Storm is cool and I enjoy his easiness.

All his talking relaxed me earlier when I was close to kicking it and saying goodbye to my future plans after I heard I'll be sharing a room with the man.

But the guy is very hooked on his girl, Kylie Bray and honestly, I don't think someone like him would ever be seen dating a homeless girl. And that bit of knowledge makes things a hell of a lot easier.

I grab the plain white t-shirt 'cause I don't think he has another color and frankly I'm tired of touching the man's condoms. The side lamp next to my bed is dim, and the orange walls make the room darker.

I don't see my nipples showing, well as long as we stay in this set up I won't. Decision made; the towel drops as I slip the shirt over my head. It falls to the top of my thighs.

I guess he forgot that I'm tall.

Screw it.

I've been dressed in less.

I pull my wet hair to the front of my face, squeezing it on the chocolate colored hardwood floor.

Once I got my hair as dry as I'm going to get it, with my foot on the now wet towel I wipe the mess up.

I spot the scissors on the tv cabinet next to the door and the thought hits me; I should cut my hair.

The last time I cut it was when I was younger and had gotten lice. My teacher took me to the change rooms after school and cut it like a boy. She also washed it plenty of times and told me that if she ever found my hair dirty like that again, she'd make sure I never saw my mother again.

Over the years, I guess I could've cut it, but a silent fuck you to Ms Coldridge was in order.

After my mother died and I left the only foster home I had, my hair became my shelter, my way to hide from the world. I always went down to the river to wash it out, so I haven't had lice since second grade.

Years went on and I just never bothered with cutting it. The comb I found in the dumpster six years ago keeps it knot free.

Combing my hair helps when the cold is unbearable and I'm starving. I normally pull my hair out and start with small sections at a time as I work out the knots. Hours go by and for that time, I forget the hunger pangs.

I know my hair is well over my butt and beyond the length for a homeless 21-year-old.

Storm said, "Nice hair," when I opened the bathroom door.

That's the first honest compliment a guy has ever given me. I have my mother's hair, it's black with loose curls only on the ends. I like my hair, it's the one thing I got of hers.

Hair cut forgotten I jump and flop on the bed just as a knock on the door comes. It's an angry hammering, shit.

"Calm down," I say to myself.

The door has a peephole and Storm is in the bathroom. He didn't lock the door.

The pounding is insistent. I slowly creep off the bed, grabbing the brass candle holder next to the phone and go to the door.

"Storm, get your ass outa there, gotta talk to the girl."

I stumble at the sound of the voice, and grab the door handle to steady myself.

The door swings open from the pressure I'm putting on the handle, at the same time Storm comes out of the bathroom like a man on a mission, but I manage to right myself just in time.

I twist my head to face Storm, who's got a towel wrapped around his waist. His hard muscles straining and dripping from the shower. His eyes cloud in anger and I follow his direction and look at the man standing at the door, Zero.

His depths rake up my body slowly, too slowly. I start to say something but before I can get a word out, Storm is in front of me, forcing me to stand behind his back.

Not sure why but I'm scared of Zero so I don't even fight Storm.

But standing behind Storm, I see a very muscular back, with a tattoo covering every inch of it with the words 'The Satan Sniper's Motorcycle Club' branded below and around the tattoo.

The sight before me makes me a little nervous.

How is it that I failed to notice he was so strong?

"I need to talk to the homeless bitch."

My chin shoots up, over Storm's shoulder and I stare smack into the face of the man that calls himself Zero. His words are meant to hurt and maybe at one time I would have felt something, but I lived too long, seen too much while surviving on scraps to let that word bother me.

It only reinforces my decision to start fresh, Storm promised to help me. I'll hold him up to that, but even if he doesn't, I'll help myself, I always have.

Zero doesn't acknowledge me. His green deep-set eyes are too focused on his brother.

The three-inch scar just under his left one makes it smaller.

If he wasn't such an asshole, I'll say he was what wild women called sexy in a bad and very dangerous way, he is however definitely not cute.

But I think the fucker is too hardcore for the sweet Falon.

He needs one of those muscle women I see leave the gym downtown.

He scares the crap out of me, and I've lived on the street.

I've faced off with evil but there is something in this man, something dark that has been leashed waiting to come out.

I pity Falon.

He doesn't look at me at all. On the streets that would mean that the man got all mouth and no balls. The smile plays on my lips at the thought. But quickly dies a dry and painful death when he does and I gulp.

"We need to talk about what happened today."

Storm moves a step to the side to block me again, he's taller than Zero so it's an easy move.

"You can talk with her once we in Kanla, with me there. She's under my protection brother. Why don't you go calm down and take care of your woman!"

"That shit isn't fuckin' happenin', something went down tonight. I wanna know what it is."

I mumble behind Storm's back. He twists his body to face me, his eyes softening.

"What did you say baby girl?"

I shoot a quick glance at Zero, who is staring blatantly at my long hair, and swallow hard. Yes fucker, look, I'm a beggar with long hair,

"I said, I want my pudding then I'll talk." Some of the tension eases out of Storm.

And Zero seems to relax somewhat.

"Can't, Venus ate it."

I go to close the door and Storm moves out of the way at the same time Zero's hand snaps out to block my movement.

"Give me ten and I'll get you another one."

I clear my throat, "Make it two, and you got a deal."

Surprise flickers in his eyes but his grim face quickly comes back into place making the scar foreboding.

I really want that pudding, so if I got to tell the scary man what happened to Falon to get it, I'm all for that.

"And hot chocolate."

He shakes his head, "Hot chocolate tomorrow and pudding today." I feel the vibration of Storm's laughter behind me. But watching Zero's hard face set on his decision, my shoulders drop. I really wished I'd thought of the hot chocolate first.

He mumbles something about bargaining but thankfully leaves the room and I shut the door wondering whether I'm going to get anything, even the pudding will do.

Storm is silent behind me. I turn to him and look up to his knowing eyes. He swallows, face full of pity.

There was a time where I wanted pity, I was sixteen and trying to get a job.

I finally got my pity in the form of a monster and the only pity he felt for me was reminding me of how I'll always be a filthy homeless beggar. How I'll always take the scraps of what people will give me. How the only pity I'll ever get was from the mercy he'd show me, none.

"I said scream beggar. SCREAM LOUDER!" His words yell in my head. I grip my temples, it's so loud.

No, not now please, not now,

"You filthy Beggar, SCREAM."

I freak out at the sound of his voice, and push Storm back against the wall.

My throat constricts. I can't breathe. Invisible fingers are squeezing my neck.

I hear Storm in the back ground, but I don't pay him any attention as I pull the door open.

Then I'm kicking it, down the narrow corridor.

I need air.

I need to feel the open space against my skin.

I need to know I'm alive, I'm free.

I can't stand pity, he pitied me, that monster.

For two days, he surely fucking pitied me.

He also showed me his pity for hours at a torturous time.

My throat is burning, my air constricting.

Storm thinks he knows me, he thinks because we've talked that he understands me. He'll never come close to feeling like me, when people like him have never known a day of hunger.

Never known the lengths a 16-year-old pregnant homeless beggar would go, to put food in her belly to feed her unborn child.

Storm's yells do nothing to help me keep those memories from attacking me.

Only my name, only one name would help me now.

And I never told him my name, I never told any of them who I am.

There's no changing that now.

The darkness of my mind is taking over, my nightmare a living reality.

The only thing I can do is let it happen, relive that which has haunted me, see his face, smell the breath I wish was retched, and feel those fingers squeezing my throat until it constricts, until my vision blurs as he rapes me, over and over,

"Scream Beggar, SCREAM."

We all have our nightmares, some smaller than others, but nightmares all the same. I just wish mine didn't feel so real.

A normal girl, someone like Falon, would've stopped to think before they ran out in a man's t-shirt and nothing else.

I'm not normal. I wished to be a normal girl, but beggars, we never get that choice.

My bare feet clap against the gravel road, the loose stones poking my hardened heels. I'm not supposed to go far, I know this, but I just keep going, I can't stop.

A chrome of metal stops in front of me, no light warning me, or maybe I run into it, I'm not sure. I stumble and fall flat on my butt, my ass cheeks get poked and bruised.

But it's a small pinch to what's happened to it before.

My breathing is heavy.

The rise and fall of my chest visible as bright lights point straight at me. My nakedness clear to see.

Instinct kicking in, I close my legs and shield my eyes with my free hand and slowly stand up.

"Wanna go for a ride?" The deep tenor voice breaks through my ears. Breaks through it all with just that demanding tone.

His words penetrating through the fog of my mind.

I can't look at him without getting blinded by his lights so I take a step to the side, out of the spotlight.

I should say no, and go back to Storm's room.

"Yeah," I agree too quickly.

Why?! I'm not sure, maybe it's because the way he asked me wasn't really a question but more of a 'you coming for a ride.' Or maybe it's the fact that I'm so scared of him that I don't think it's a good idea to say no to a big broody biker that can snap me in half without much effort.

I just know I'm going for a ride with this green-eyed man.

I stand there without moving, aware of the dirt stuck on the cheeks of my ass and small stones still embedded on my palms. I don't dust it off, I'm too stunned to do anything by what this man had just done.

"I don't got all day." He drawls the words out, rolling it over his tongue.

Something peeks out between his teeth. I think it's one of those tongue piercings. I walk closer to him, mindful that Storm isn't chasing after me anymore.

"I don't got any panties," I shoot back.

He's quiet and so still and I'm thinking maybe I shouldn't have said that. But he throws his head back and laughs, his face transforms as it crinkles around his eyes and pulls around his cheeks. The man has a really nice laugh. My lips tug, and for the first time I get on the back of Zero's bike.

My arms wrapped around his cut, hair tucked in the t-shirt I'm wearing. My cheek on his back. My legs brushing his denim clad thighs.

The engines roar going straight to my core and the heat of his machine warming my naked one. I welcome the motor fumes into my lungs, and the light essence of Zero's manly scent.

My mind blanks by the hum of the engine. I'm not aware of much until I feel Zero's fingers grip my thighs just above my knees. He pulls me roughly, my ass dragged on the leather seat until my hips are plastered to his back. Zero throttles the engine, as if he didn't just shatter me with that one innocent touch.

He's taking it fast. My body moving with his to the glide and drop of the machine. And for a second, I swear I'm flying.

The wind blows through the thin material that does little to hide me and I come alive.

I'm seen. For the first time I'm actually seen, not as a beggar but a human.

It's too soon that we come across a service station. I expect him to leave me by the motorcycle and cringe when I see how stupid I am. He will be leaving me with nothing on besides Storm's t-shirt.

My nipples are still poking from the cold when he stops. The lights force my eyes to squint. And I can only imagine how dreadful I must look.

He sees my outfit, and also my predicament. The eye with the scar twitches, getting smaller and angry in the light.

I gulp, I'm feeling something, I'm just not sure what, but it's making me want to run, and get away, far away.

Without thinking he slips his cut off and hands it to me.

I say without thinking, because there's no way a biker who is thinking clearly would be giving me his cut.

I'm street smart, I know he shouldn't be giving me this. It's a symbol, something only your woman wears.

I push it back crossing my arms over my chest, my throat raspy,

"Nah, you keep it, I don't want no trouble with Falon."

Something crosses his features but he covers it and that hardness I have seen since I've met him returns. So does the fear, *my fear* for this man.

"Woman, you better put the jacket on and let me decide who wears my fuckin' clothes."

My knees quiver as I slip his cut on without another word when he opens it for me. I know when to choose my battles.

If he wants to belittle his woman for the likes of me, I'm not going to fight him. I'm not just saying that because I'm shit scared of the scary biker.

We go into the shop together and I duck my head down when I hear some assholes whistle.

Not because of my dignity, I lost that a long time ago. It's because I don't want them to piss off the bad biker next to me.

After a very tense ten minutes and moody Zero with no hot chocolate, (they didn't sell any), we're back on the road to the Inn.

I don't say anything when I get off Zero's bike 20 minutes later. I take the leather cut off my warm body and hand it back to him. The chill of the night kisses my skin, reminding me of who I am, a beggar.

Zero is silent as well.

His burning gaze and the graze of his fingers when he takes his cut from my outstretched hand, screams that I should run. It's taking everything in me not to kick it as he slips the leather on to where it belongs, on him.

"What's your name?"

I breathe in deeper at the question. A bead sticks out between his teeth, it's gone again as he waits for me to answer.

I keep my eyes up, concentrating on his black mass of hair in the center of his head that hasn't been shaven off like the sides. His hand glides through it, keeping the hair out of his face.

The same fingers rub his jaw and then that scarred eye as it gets smaller. My fear for him returns with a vengeance. I skid across the parking lot knowing my private parts are covered because I have been this naked before, and even if it wasn't, I really just want to get away from this biker.

The packet in my hand knocks my knee reminding me of what I promised, reminding me that I'm not getting away from the biker yet.

He follows close behind me.

"Can you stop running and talk to me, I know nothing about you."

"I'm twenty-one," I huff out, dryly, "Born December 8th, lived on the streets of Washington my whole life, that's all you need to know about me."

I don't think I spoke so much in one sentence since I turned seventeen, that was years ago.

My throat got damaged years back. Spending four days constantly screaming, did that to me. I screamed until my vocal cords were permanently damaged.

When I escaped, or got rescued, depending on who asks, the risk involved in getting medical attention was too great. I wasn't getting caught, no way. So, I just kept my mouth shut. Nobody wants to hear the beggar talking anyway.

"I need more than that, tell me your name," He insists.

I walk down the corridor to the room I'm sharing with Storm.

Zero's boots keep up behind me.

"I'm still thinking about it," I say honestly.

My hand pounds the door twice before it swings open and Storm appears from the other side dressed in a white t-shirt similar to the one, I'm wearing and blue checkered boxers.

The smile on his lips when he sees my grip on the packet is a relief.

Zero touches my lower back and I run into the room as if he burnt me, which he might as well have, fucker.

That's three times in one day.

Three times he has touched me. He doesn't know that I don't like to be touched and I'm not sure why I haven't said anything the first time.

I don't say anything about it now either and neither does Storm.

I sit on the end of the bed and rummage through my packet. My mouth watering for the sweet goodies.

I look up only when I get my first taste of the chocolate and berry pudding. The flavor bursts in my mouth, forcing a groan from my throat.

Zero plants his butt on the dresser chair and Storm stands behind him. Both men staring at me for entirely different reasons. Storm's mouth is hanging open, his arms crossed over his chest, probably wondering if I'll offer.

Zero has his hands locked in the front of his pants, no doubt talking himself out of strangling me.

I carry on eating knowing full well that they're watching me, but I ain't offering them shit. This pudding is delicious, best damn thing I've ever eaten.

Zero clears his throat.

"It's three in the morning girl. We gotta be up at six. I ain't got all day."

I drop my head after my first pudding is finished and slide myself up the bed and into the covers. My second pudding forgotten for now and my body covered I clear my tortured throat.

"Let's see, uhm, yeah, your girl was on the phone, I think with you."

I peep at Zero for confirmation which he doesn't give.

His face is completely blank. Nothing.

I swallow the thick saliva lodged in my throat from the pudding,

"I was between the dumpsters waiting for the club to close."

"Why?" Storm is the one to ask.

I pull my hair over my neck, eyes on the orange floral blanket.

"The owner promised me a hot meal if I spoke with him after they closed."

Both of them say nothing and my vision involuntarily rises to the scary bikers. Zero has a death glare and Storm's eyes are clouded in something that's making me wish I ran the other way.

Shit, I don't think they want to be hearing about me. They wanna know about that sweet girl.

"Falon walked further away," I rush out, "I didn't hear her fo.."

"Hold the fuck on a minute!" My hands start shaking in my lap at the cold tone of Zero's order.

"You just agreed to meet this fucker." Storm says in a bare whisper like he can't believe it.

My skin flames red in anger,

"He promised me a hot meal, I never had a hot meal," I shoot back in my defense.

They both quieten.

And my small anger evaporates,

"So, you wanna know what happened to your girl or not? I don't want Storm falling off his bike while I'm on the back." I don't look at them, I refuse to see their pity and sad faces when they don't know shit.

They think they do, but they don't.

"Tell me."

With those two words I don't even know who spoke it. I begin and I don't disappoint and they don't interrupt.

I tell them what they want to know, and I don't stop until both men that harmed their sweet Falon is on the floor, dead.

The two bikers don't ask any questions after that.

They don't say a thing.

Both quiet.

My throat pains from all that talking. I don't look up to see their faces. I don't wanna know what they're thinking. Instead I keep my face blank and pretend I don't exist.

When they both leave the room and the lock on the door clicks, I let out a huff, and allow that cold feeling to seep through me for just a moment, the feeling I had accustomed myself to over the years. The feeling one gets after taking a life.

My eyes droop and I fall asleep, snuggled under the covers.

A warm bed to rest on for the first time in years.

VI

I t's closing on midnight when we finally get to the Clubhouse. The iron rooted gates open and all the brothers file in, stopping in their parking spaces. I'm last to get in, Falon nice and snug to my back.

I park my V-Rod next to Killer's red Dyna just as the man jogs down the porch steps.

The cold creeps in on my back when Falon gets off and rushes past Killer without a word.

Most probably to go lay down.

Her stomach has been cramping since the morning. And my guilt of not being able to help her has played on my mind since we got on my bike this morning.

I tried talking to my woman before we left the Inn and again when we stopped for gas but she shut me out.

I didn't understand it. My first thought was maybe someone said something about my trip with a certain girl last night.

But I know my family.

Still didn't explain why she barely spoke ten words to me in the past 16 hours.

"What took you motherfuckers so long." Killer hits my back and moves on to the others.

I give him no response, he's aware of the situation. Killer is the fastest thinker among all of us. Rounder thinks he's just a soldier but the brother is much more than that.

We don't like keeping shit from our President but since we found out Rounder has cancer, the brothers and I agreed that we needed someone protecting the man.

Killer was the choice we voted on and he lives up to his name. I'm not sure why he became a Satan Sniper. But he is, and he's a damn good brother. Which was why I called him first after we got all the details of what happened with Falon.

I pull Falon's bag out from my bike and trek to the face brick four story farm house we use as our Clubhouse and home.

Compliments of the government.

It was a small passing gift they gave us two years ago. But we took it for what it truly was. They were letting us know that they knew where we stayed. Like giving us their blessing but informing us that they still own most of us. We took it, obviously.

We never turn shit down from our bosses if we want peace and they were wise not to bug it.

The land is fifty acres of utter bliss with a lake, forest and space. Lots of space. The high steel enforced; brick camouflaged walls were one of the many changes we added ourselves. For security purposes of course.

"I thought you said small." I catch the easily recognizable voice a few meters away.

I turn around to see her, my foot on the second step of the polished porch. One hand in my back pocket, the other holding Falon's bag.

She's in deep conversation with Storm and Killer and got that fucking jacket on again, hiding her face under the hood.

I still can't drop my eyes, hood or not.

The sight of her naked under that fucking t-shirt and the feel of her thighs under my fingers are too fresh not to remember, too present to look away.

The girl is dangerous and she doesn't even have a clue.

And for the first time since I met her, I'm wondering what the fuck I'm doing.

She's a homeless 21-year-old. Way too young for me and even more fucked up than I presumed.

After she told me what happened with Falon, I wished I knew sooner.

I should've made her tell me before I decided to get her on the back of my bike. Before I broke so many laws giving her my cut when I had my President's daughter, the woman I intend to claim as mine, wounded in a bed after almost getting raped.

I used the situation as an excuse to talk to the homeless girl, find out her name. I was the one who hunted her down when Storm was right, I should have been with Falon coaxing it out of her.

There's no way I'm going to screw things up with Falon for some homeless girl I met in an alley with a gun in her hand.

The Enforcer in me wanted to kill those men again, more painfully. Storm agreed, when I voiced this,

"Those fuckers died too easily."

I had no words for the girl with the broken voice after all she had confessed.

She sure as shit didn't have anything else to say either.

Storm and I both watched her this morning, waiting for her to look at us after she had finished filling in the blanks about what happened at Lazers.

I wanted her to notice that I was there for her when the other shoe dropped.

It didn't.

Both of us stood still thinking similar thoughts, maybe she'll scream, or cry, rant or rave, something to release that hollowness that plagued a person after they took a life.

She didn't, nothing happened.

Something switched off in her, she became so still and frozen, hoping we'll forget she was in the room, forget that she killed those guys and admitted it without a hitch in her tone.

I'm glad I saw it sooner than later. It only concreted my decision that I won't let this girl come between Falon and me.

My feet move to the Clubhouse doors, the smell of disinfectant hits my nose and I'm glad to be home.

The 16-seater set of Red custom-made leather couches greet me silently as I pass them turning the corner and going toward the bar.

We bought the couches last year when the last set was infested with ants. In fact, we refurbished the whole Clubhouse after that diabolical event.

I ignore the loud calls and laughs happening outside and decide to go through the empty hall space straight to the stairs that lead to the bedrooms instead.

Spotting Snake sitting on the feeding counter in front of the liquor cabinet, I do however make a U-turn.

"Yo slither."

The side of his face with the small snakes tattooed on it lifts up into a devil's grin,

"Yo. I started thinking you guys stopped in Houston." He lifts his head up from the piles of paper work he's doing.

I shrug and drop Falon's bag on the floor,

"We had to stop more than intended brother. Falon wasn't doing too good."

He frowns, and nods in understanding.

"Saw her run by, might wanna let Prez know his girl's back, he was up the whole night, Killer had to knock his ass out." Cringing at the same time I grimace he gestures to the closed door opposite the staircase.

"Gotta see to Falon first man." Is all I say before I'm walking in the opposite direction and up the carpeted stairs.

When I get to Falon's room, I brace myself before I open the door. I expect to see her laying down, or throwing up.

I'm beyond shocked, when I see her small frame spread eagle on the four-poster bed, naked.

Her white sheets crinkled.

Two dainty fingers lodged in her pussy, finger fucking her cunt. I can see her arousal from the door way. Wet and glistening.

Her eyes hooded with a need I've come to know as she looks at me.

My cock stirs, and all my thoughts take a backseat.

"Add another finger, you know my cocks much bigger baby."

I close the door at the same time she puts a third finger inside her wetness.

My steps bring me closer to her and my cock gets harder at wanting to play.

It's an hour later. We're in the shower, two condoms less when I realize I'm not satisfied. I need more, I want more.

When Falon moves to get out of the shower, I grab her by the hips and hoist her up on to the wet shower walls. My tongue grazing hers and I close my eyes, giving her nothing too deep.

I grind my cock against her pussy and she eagerly responds.

I drop her gently on her feet and tug her hair down with my left hand, careful to keep my back against the shower streams.

"Get on your knees," I bite out.

She goes happily and takes me into her mouth, just how I like, paying close attention to the tip.

I've never fucked Falon raw or any woman for that matter. I use my own condoms, no pulling out, or taking pills. I wrap it or leave it.

I don't want any kids popping up and getting trapped into a marriage I don't want. Or my kid growing up a bastard.

My parents got married because my mama fell pregnant with my blood brother, Thorn.

They despised each other right up till dad fucked Tonia, a prospect of The Satan Snipers at the time, now a booker for the Houston Chapter.

She fell pregnant with twins. He ditched my mama so fast. Took Thorn and me with him.

He didn't marry Tonia and lucky he didn't, she miscarried at four months.

My mama didn't take the news of my father's infidelity and the divorce well but didn't fight for us either. She was glad to be rid of us, in fact she seemed relieved.

Didn't want no weekends, nothing.

I haven't seen her in sixteen years and neither has Thorn.

My dad is a great father, doesn't mean I want to repeat his shit. So, until I marry Falon, I'm not taking any chances.

I know she wants to take that step, but I can't.

It's something I have never been willing to risk for any woman.

Even now with Fallon's hot mouth sucking me down her throat and my eyes rolled back I will never make that mistake.

VII

We've been at the Clubhouse for an hour. Bull, Knight and Venus have since moved to the kitchen for half that time, preparing food. Chadley, Storm, Spade and Texas are setting the 24-seater black wood dining table I'm currently seated by.

Where are the others? I'm not sure. I'm just glad we got here, finally.

I haven't met the president yet, but Storm was kind enough to introduce me to the others.

I'm good with names so I caught on quickly which earned me some points from the guys.

The girls seem harder to crack, they haven't uttered much to me since we met.

I think it's because of Wisp. I'm hoping they'll change their minds. I wasn't talking smack when I said I don't want any problems.

What I'm hoping these biker girls would figure out soon is, I don't want a man more.

"Yo girly girl, you want steak or sausage." My head snaps up to see who's talking and to who. It's Knight and he's talking to me.

I pull my hoody down. Knowing it's rude to keep it on any longer.

"Which ones tastier?"

He stares at me, not saying anything for a moment, then snaps out of whatever's got him stuck,

"Steak it is."

Killer, the guy that I met earlier who doesn't match the others, (he is just too refined) comes from behind the corner which is the lounge area and hits Knight on the back. He does that to a lot of the guys.

"Don't be greedy asshole, give the girl both." He gives me a bright smile that I'm sure has gotten many women naked in the past wondering what the hell did they just do.

But those blue eyes and light brown hair doesn't fool me. I've lived in danger, breathed it, I know a devil when I see one.

"You doing okay there, new girl?"

"Ask me that after I get that steak."

Knight smiles and Killer gives me a strange look, before shaking his head.

"Will do."

Knight goes back into the kitchen area that is closed by two double doors at the same time Venus comes through, a tray in her hand filled with at least three dozen rolls.

Her face is flushed and her purple eyes are red from lack of sleep, but she's still a beauty. Her light brown hair now tied up in a messy bun is almost as long as mine. She's everything a girl like me would never be.

"Help yourself, the margarine is there." Even her voice is soft and sweet.

"Thanks Venus."

I almost flinch at how I must stick out like a sore thumb, more so with my fucked-up voice but stop myself when she gives me a genuine bright smile.

I take the roll and stick it in my mouth.

Killer sits directly opposite me mimicking my actions.

My brow arches in confusion, he does the same.

My mouth moves slowly, chewing the roll when I really want to shove it down quickly and get another.

He moans but still mirrors my actions until I swallow.

"So. My boy Storm tells me you got a thing about people knowing your name, you got something to hide girl."

I'm stunned, and my heart begins to pick up speed.

Just a second ago he was sitting there, copying my actions like it's the easiest thing to do.

Now he's all serious, except he makes it so cool.

Who the fuck is this guy?

For the first time since Killer sat down, I look around. All the others are gone, leaving the two of us alone, fuck.

I've never gotten distracted before. When you live on the streets a weak moment is all you need to get you in trouble and it's not because of the homeless folk like me.

There are much worse predators lurking around.

Take Falon for example. Multiply that by a hundred because I actually lived on the streets my whole life.

It took Falon a few minutes of not paying attention to land herself in trouble and she was barely outside for ten minutes.

So, it's in my nature to take stock of my surroundings.

This guy is dangerous, and though my senses tell me Falon's man is the one I should fear. My mind tells me the true demon in this club comes with blue eyes that are meant to lower your guard, and a smile to entrap you with its beauty.

Who just happens to be sitting across from me!

Killer's body is relaxed on the chair. The half-eaten roll still in his hand and gaze trained on me.

And me? I'm frozen in place.

The air is getting thicker, and it's me who's the cause.

There are so many people in this place yet no one comes to interrupt us, why?!

I shove the rest of my roll in my mouth. Some of it sticking out.

I'm not certain what I expect him to do but shoving his roll in his own mouth isn't one of them.

After some serious chewing I swallow at the same time he does, and I can't hold it in, I laugh, it's one of those fear mangled nervous laughs. It picks up because of my gruff voice and Killer joins me.

We both laugh like crazy-people for entirely different reasons.

Me? well, I do have stuff to hide and we both know it.

Why he's laughing I have no fucking clue, but it's real loud.

Knight walks in carrying a big tray with delicious steam coming from it. He takes in the scene, his brown eyed stare widening a fraction. The long- haired biker turns his head to Killer, giving me a glimpse of the snake head tattooed to his neck.

Those red eyes snap my mouth shut.

Killer quietens too, but I don't look at the devil in disguise.

I'm too chicken to chance a glance and have him bring up any more questions.

Heaven knows I know when to shut my yap and bow my head. After all, I've done it my whole life.

I should've known that he isn't going to drop it.

"Listen, I don't want you to feel like I'm pressuring you. I just asked a question. But fare enough you not ready to talk, fine. But you need a name. Something."

The sound of footsteps behind me slow down.

Knight puts the food on the table as Venus and the big muscular guy, Bull, walks in holding bottles of Coca-Cola and packs of beer.

Chadley, Spade, Wisp and Texas sit down in the empty spaces down from Killer, who is still watching me.

Storm plants himself next to me without saying a word.

They are all quiet.

I turn to Storm, his amber eyes expectant.

Shit, they want a name.

I look to the food in the middle of the table. The steak and sausages make my mouth water.

A chair scrapes on the end and I follow the sound to see Zero. He doesn't glance at me as he pulls out the black chair.

Falon drops in it without a sound besides Zero scraping it in.

She looks freshly showered and so does he, the knowledge as to why, causes a panic to overcome me.

I'm not sure why. My throat feels tighter and I claw at it, my blunt nails scraping the skin around my neck.

"No." Zero's deep volcanic voice coming from across the room silences my head enough to see a frail older man walking toward us.

I inhale and tell myself I'm okay, the monster is gone.

And although my mind is fighting to go to its dark place, I'm able to hold it back by that simple command.

Another girl's face would've turned Crimson and blushed, maybe even felt embarrassed by her actions and left.

I'm not like that, those emotions were raped from me, mind, body and spirit. I can't feel them.

Sometimes I ask myself if I put a bullet in my leg would I even cry. It's like I'm dead inside.

Except last night on the back of Zero's bike, I felt something breathe life in me.

I have no idea what it is but it's scary. I don't trust scary.

The only scary I've known came in a 6 foot three package that promised only goodness in a fancy car.

I unwrapped it like the hard-up eager naïve teenager I was. And it turned out to be a big fucking Monster that didn't just give me bad dreams but live fucking nightmares that still haunts me years after, wherever I go, reminding me that demons always come in the most appealing of packages.

"If you gotta choose a name what will it be?" Killer asks, unaffected by the audience and my obvious inner battle I have going on inside me.

My eyes snap off the older man walking closer to us and to Killer's blue all-knowing gaze.

I clear my throat,

"Why do I need a name?"

He shrugs, with a tilt of his head like he can see deep within me,

"What will we call you if you don't have one?"

I glance across the table and everyone's eyes are on me, apart from one, Zero and it bothers me.

Why the fuck does it bother me? I should be relieved but I'm not. The older man who must be the President stands behind his chair, and gives me an encouraging nod.

I turn my head to Storm giving me his undivided attention.

"Ah," I swallow, my throat is dry, eyes back on Killer,

"How about?"

Killer arches his left brow as patient as ever, fucker,

"Yes?"

My palms get sweaty, I think fuck it.

They are either going to accept me or not.

This is who I am, this is me.

Taking one last breath, I look straight into Killers eyes and say

"Beggar."

I say it loud enough that they can all hear me.

Killer is quiet and my confidence increases knowing that I managed to shut the devil up.

"Fuck, I didn't see that one coming," He cringes and my lip tugs.

"You sure." I turn my head to Storm's question.

"Yeah, Beggar," I say, my tone firm.

Storm's lips thin showing his displeasure but he doesn't say anything else and I'm glad. He proceeds to lift my plate up and starts dishing me steak and sausage. My mouth salivates as my vision feasts on the yummy meat I'm about to eat.

"Choose something else." I miss the low voice, but my eyes immediately shoot to the owner, Zero, who won't look at me but his grip around the fork and hard line of his lips inform me that it's a good thing he doesn't.

"No." I give him his word back.

Knight sighs, "Zero's right, it doesn't feel right calling you that, girly girl."

I hear the other males grunt and mumble, but the women are quiet.

My plate lands in front of me and I pick the steak up and bite into it.

It's so fucking good, my mouth tingles as I chew. The flavor is indescribable, I have nothing to compare it to.

I never had a hot meal, well now I have.

I take another bite and block the group out, knowing the whole crew is watching me.

When someone's throat clears, I face the Italian, who calls himself Knight.

"It's my name, the only one." My words are terse and to the point.

I don't want them complaining about it while I'm enjoying my first hot meal. The muttered curse from one of the girls doesn't faze me.

"Well Beggar." I turn my head to the sound of the voice, Rounder. "Welcome to The Satan Sniper's Motorcycle Club."

Rounder's painful eyes crease into a weak smile and the balding head bends in acknowledgment.

I'm grateful and am familiar with the drill. Once the boss talks, they're all screwed because he accepted it, he accepted my name.

I nod back, "Thank you Prez."

"Thank you, Beggar." The grimace when he says my name doesn't go unnoticed.

Storm coughs and Venus bursts out laughing.

The air around us is still intense, many of the guys aren't happy. But fuck them, it's my name. I wasn't lying when I told them that's my name, at least the one I gave myself four years ago.

I blow it off and grab a roll just as the others start filling their plates. I take my sausage and place it in the center of the roll and shove it in my mouth.

Zero's eyes are on me, I can feel it, and it takes everything in me not to duck under the table just to get away from his cold stare.

He should be focusing on Falon not looking at me. He's an idiot, an arrogant, bossy idiot.

"You want another piece?" My eyes shoot up from my plate to Storm, who's holding a steak mid-air with a fork,

"God yes."

He dumps it on my plate and licks his fingers.

Killer starts up a conversation with Texas about football and puts another roll in my plate without taking his eyes off his brother.

Ten minutes later I'm done. My stomach is full.

Killer turns his attention off Texas to me,

"You doing okay there, new girl?"

I smile and shake my head, "Best fucking meal ever."

My words must have had importance to him because he rubs his jaw and nods like I just answered an important question.

Fuck, If I care, I didn't even finish school.

VIII

Today is a new day, a new week. For many of us it's a fresh start over, following the weekend. But for some it's just another fucked up day reminding us of what we lost, what we gained and what we want but will never have.

Such is life.

For my brother Bull it's the second.

His dark grey eyes that once creased whenever he smiled, which used to be every fucking time, now pointed to the cemented basement floor as if it had all the fucking answers to why his life turned out so wrong.

Why did he lose the one thing he wanted for years, yet only got two months with? His dead wife, Nakita.

At 33 and 6 feet of solid muscle, not to mention the biggest guy in the club, including our Mother chapter in Houston, you'd think a man like him would've moved on, or at least found a woman to warm his bed.

But he doesn't touch any of the girls. They all offered, he just doesn't give a crap.

My eyes settle to what he does give a crap about, that's dangling from his hand, weed.

He smokes 24/7.

I don't mind it now and again. I ain't judging but for a guy who is road captain and spends majority of his time handling our trips it's dangerous, meaning I got to keep an extra eye on him.

I don't like it but a part of me understands.

"Put that fuckin' shit out, it's the fuckin' morning brother. Jesus fuck." Killer however doesn't. He's the only one. But then again that's who he is.

Bull pinches the end of the joint so quickly, I feel bad for the man.

Killer is one brother you don't push, especially in the morning.

The basement is our place where we handle church.

A year back we installed a handprint security to the entry door. No unwanted guests allowed.

Unless you one of us, and I mean a full patch member, only then you can enter. It was Killer and Storm's idea. Best thing ever invented.

Venus walks in carrying three coffee mugs on a tray. She hands me mine, a black sugarless delight. I inhale my coffee bean medicine.

Snake takes his and saddles next to me on the wheeled office chair he purchased last Christmas. One for each of us.

"Checked out the new girl. Cute. Gave her kitchen duty. She doesn't look like no beggar to me man."

I grunt.

The scar under my eye pulls taut at the mention of her. Shit, I need to get my head out of the gutter, literally.

This morning was a new day. A good day. Had my cock sucked by my woman, then had fine pussy also from my woman.

Beggar wasn't even on my mind. She wasn't even a thought.

"Beggar, ha, out of all the damn names in this world she chose Beggar, might as well tattoo I'm stupid on her fucking forehead."

"She ain't stupid asshole," Storm glares from across me.

I swallow a sip of coffee, realizing I just said that shit loud. But I'm not going to regret it, fuck no, they don't call me Zero for nothing.

"You know she's actually lived on the street her whole life, you telling me she went to school."

Storm's nostrils flare, his jaw practically ready to pop and I don't fucking like it.

I put my cup on the table on the left. Pinning him down with my narrowed glare. VP or not I've had enough of his shit.

"Enough both of you."

We both turn our heads to the fading man we call our President. I resume my position as before and pick up the red mug with my coffee. Storm doesn't look at me after that and I do the same.

Once the room quietens, I turn behind me to see if the others have arrived.

The basement has two windows, one above Bulls head, the other on top of Knight and Venus who are sitting close to the steps next to the three freezers we keep our meat in.

My vision darts past the blue painted walls, Texas who's wearing his cowboy hat, and Spade saddled next to him one row up from me, until it stops on Killer.

He's partially hidden in the shadows. Just like me. But I sit down. He has one leg on the wall, his face an impenetrable mask.

Killer is way younger than all of us in this room at just 23. But his eyes say they're ancient.

He served his country at eighteen, joined the navy at just sixteen became a special ops member at 20.

I play with my tongue ring as I stare at him, ignoring the other voices.

He's fully dressed this morning, lip ring, eyebrow piercings. The thought makes me smile.

Yesterday Beggar must've fell for his charm as many did, but Today she'll meet the Killer.

She'll be running back to the streets soon enough. Where she belongs.

The thought leaves a foul taste in my mouth. I know I'm talking crap. I wouldn't let her get as far as the front gate.

Killer drops his leg and takes a step into the light, his arms cross over his black t-shirt chest and smirks at me.

I ignore him, with a shake of my head and focus on the Prez. I can't help it, I like the kid.

Rounder pierces the knife in the black oak table signaling church in session. We all straighten to face him, except of course Storm who moves to the vacant seat next to Prez.

I slip my cut on, and so does all the others.

"Did the girl sleep good?" Rounder asks to no one in particular.

"Yup, got her next to Zero's room down the hall." Venus answers.

"Let's cut to the chase, Beggar saved Falon's life, and from what Killer says, also saved my babies pride, now that shit is an act of a true Satan Sniper.

We need people like her. So we vote.

The choices are simple, she either gets patched in first then undergoes training. Or she prospects and becomes a member after.

The third option, and this one I thought about but disagree with, is we set her up with a job and give her a place of her own."

His body racks with a series of coughs as he finishes.

Venus walks over and gives him a bottle of water from the packs on the floor near the freezers.

I watch his eyes soften at the Doctor. It's hard watching him fade away.

Rounder has been our man, our leader since forever. When he decided he wanted to move here, we didn't question him, we just followed.

I've served under him in Iraq and on ops all over the world. It's a shame to see him come to this.

"We don't know anything about her. I have Snake looking into her, so far, he got nothing, it's almost like she doesn't exist. But we'll find something."

He clears his throat, after handing us that bit of information. That sound isn't too good, in fact it's bad, very fucking bad.

"Let's vote." Rounder says in a phlegm filled voice.

Ten minutes later the Prez has his answers.

"Bull, Texas, Killer, Venus, Spade and Storm voted no to full member." He hits his chest, reading on.

"Zero suggests a job and partial hang on."

The Prez locks me with a fuming stare, his teeth grinding together,

"She saved my daughter."

Yeah, if he was his full self, I'll be under his boot by now.

"She can barely stand to be touched, how is she going to go through the program? I'm not comfortable training her in combat if she's going to freak every time, I touch her." Spade voices this from behind me.

I'm not surprised he got there without me hearing it. He loves sitting in the same seat. Next to the stairs.

"Afraid she'll hurt your balls?" That comes from Snake.

"Nah man, I'll lose them." They all laugh at that, even the Prez.

Killer walks closer in.

"I could do it," He suggests rubbing the back of his neck.

"Say what?" I ask.

He rolls his eyes and walks to the vacant chair next to Snake,

"When I took her upstairs, she asked me to wait for her to sleep. She was thrashing and shit, then woke up. Told me I could touch her then went back to sleep."

The thought sends fury like nothing else to overcloud rational thought. Why, I don't care.

"She went back to sleep? That's it?" The accusatory is full in my question.

His attention stays above Rounders head, refusing to look at me. He doesn't answer. Just gets up to hide in the shadows.

Killer's lying, something went down.

And he ain't gonna tell me shit.

I can't go beating his ass for it either.

He got the name Killer in the Navy at 19 and it's not because of his blue eyes and killer looks as Chadley likes to believe.

The others are quiet. Thinking the same thought as me.

"What did Venus vote?" Bulls deep rusty voice fills the room.

"A full member. Prospect and a paying job." Rounder answers.

"Explain." Storm demands.

Venus moves to the front. Giving the males a perfect view of her luscious ass snugged in painted-on black denims, and a blue vest showing the shape of her round tits.

I had it, tasted it and fucked it.

There was no connection between Venus and I besides a deep-rooted friendship, didn't mean we didn't enjoy each other.

She's one of the very few females patched in members of the club. She's also our doctor and not just medical doctor but our psychologist.

We all perk up to hear what the Doc has to say.

"She passed the ultimate test of the club so she deserves to be a member. If we bend the rules now because she's a homeless girl, what does that say about us?"

"Tell them babe." Spade chortles.

The glares he receives from Storm and the Prez makes me wanna laugh. I could feel the blonde-haired soldier gulp.

Spade likes to mess around and is easy to be around but like Killer, his blue eyes and easy-going nature is just a mask.

He can snap a guy's neck in less than ten seconds.

I've witnessed his murderous nature.

He was kicked out of the squad a year ago due to unstable mental behavior.

And branded too dangerous for missions.

At 29 he's a retired USA veteran and a full pledged contract sniper for the club.

We don't believe he is unfit for work. We all know that he faked the whole thing to get off the squad.

It was his grandmas dying wish.

"As I was saying," Venus continues, "She deserves to be a member, but that doesn't mean we got to just hand it to her. Plus, I think psychologically a job and a purpose will be good for Beggar."

"What's your take on her mental state?" Storm asks.

She tucks a loose hair behind her ear, her well-shaped brows frown,

"I don't think she's unstable. More so than a lot of people in this room." Her front faces the rest of us and her violet eyes find mine, and I hold her stare until she turns back to face the Prez.

"It's obvious that she has some bad memories but I think it's one memory.

Something triggers it and she has a panic attack. Which is totally normal considering her circumstances!"

"It's only men she seems to have issues with. I think the women are ok." Storm voices.

"I noticed earlier when Zero commanded her, she instantly reacted." Venus says.

"Like a switch. Could mean she's submissive," Killer walks out of his shadow.

"Or had a really fucked up experience with a man or men." Knight suggests.

Which I got to admit makes sense.

"She was definitely raped or tortured somehow. And found a coping mechanism by suppressing her experience. I'm sure you all know what happens when you choose not to confront your past." Venus says, turning to face the rest of us.

"It becomes a living breathing demon." The soft words from Bull makes me cringe.

If there's anyone who could relate it'll be him.

"Question is how do we help her?" Rounder asks the question I want to know.

"We can't, she's going to have to help herself. We could be there and offer her comfort and family but ultimately the only person who can help Beggar is herself."

"Shit." Storm mutters.

"How about forcing her to face her demons." I ask before I could help myself.

"It could work, but getting her to do it, to talk about stuff is going to take trust. A lot of trust. And a girl with a background like hers isn't going to open her heart and soul to anyone."

"Who said anything about having a choice?" I say.

"Let Zero and I train her for now," Killer suggests, now standing right in front of the Prez, his teeth in his lip ring.

I don't like the eager expression he doesn't bother to suppress.

"She's comfortable around Storm," Venus interjects.

"Too comfortable, I'm a Sadist, and she's submissive. I know what I'm doing," Killer counters.

Venus purses her lips together eyes narrowing on Killer,

"I can't tell you what to do. You gonna do what you wanna do anyway."

"Thanks for the confidence, but the jealousy is really uncalled for."

She fumes, "Beggar is a nice girl, she doesn't need your dose of fucked upness along with Zero's."

"Hey," I warn standing up.

"Everyone sit the fuck down," Rounder says and starts coughing.

"Zero can take the first day, alone. Then Killer. She needs the girls to make her feel welcome, don't like the way you women sat away from her. She won't feel welcome until then. So, do whatever you got to do, force them, I don't give a shit, but by the end of today I want that girl feeling welcomed. There's enough dicks here for all of you to share."

"That's gonna be hard." Texas explains, "Wisp ain't feeling very welcoming to Miss Beggar."

"Too fuckin' bad. I might be sick but I'm still the fucking President, she better get fuckin' welcoming fast or she'll be pulling doubles this weekend."

We talk about other club business and the murders.

Jade's departure to Houston is a concern for the brothers 'cause her sister is still missing.

We discuss a few new contracts.

All the while I'm asking myself why the fuck ain't I claiming Falon.

I said I would, but something is holding me back. And I know what it is. A pair of black dead eyes.

IX

I listen to my brothers speaking, I listen to Venus. But I can't focus.

My mind and my body are absent. It's still stuck in the early hours of the morning replaying the previous hours alone with Beggar. Watching her while she slept.

She resembled a porcelain doll with small cracks, begging to be put together, begging to be saved.

It's no secret that I have lived in luxury. I've lived with riches my entire life. I've never wanted, never needed. Until I left home. Until I decided that I just didn't fit with my brothers and sisters back home in Liston Hills.

I was always different. A fast thinker, sure, but not business minded like my siblings.

I didn't see myself living in a high-rise building, wearing a 5-thousand-dollar suit. I don't see myself as Kevin Stone either, son of billionaire Hector Stone.

And maybe my dad didn't see it too, because he didn't stop me when I decided to join the Navy. He didn't say a thing when I decided to become a Satan Sniper.

My mother wasn't thrilled, but she's my mother, she wished me well and just wanted me to be happy. But truth is, I'm not happy. I've never really felt anything.

When I joined the Elite special ops, I didn't get the training the other guys went through to suppress their emotion. I didn't need it.

I was born this way.

The army said every few years if they got lucky, they would find someone like me. I know Texas is one of those 'someone'. And like him, I smile, when I need to smile. I joke when I should, but everything is planned out, everything is a big game.

Only I'm the main player, the one who already knows all the moves. Bending, twisting, turning, and eliminating when the time deems.

When I saw Beggar, she was covered with a hoody.

Her actions screamed fear. But like every new piece I managed to see the cracks.

She let her guard down in teasing peeks, giving me insight of the girl, she is, was.

Not the broken fragile one, these people make her out to be, a girl haunted by a memory. But the one who killed those men in the alley, the fearless female who would do anything to survive, anything to see that no girl meets her faith.

I saw the girl who survived her entire life on the streets, I saw Beggar. I understand why she chose the name.

Why she chose the hoody.

But there is so much more to her. Beggar is a contradiction. She can't stand the touch of a male. Yet she chanced secret stares to Zero when he wasn't paying attention.

It didn't go as unnoticed as she hoped to. Nor the ones she chanced to me.

I replay the scene that caused my turmoil.

"Thanks." Her rusty, broken voice cuts the silence.

I stand by the door of her room and watch her pale skin. No flush or embarrassment reddens her pale cheeks.

Her black beaded eyes that I will, for years to come, always compare to my sister's porcelain dolls, widen when I go to close the door.

"Stop, stay until I fall asleep," She rasps.

My response is to refuse, but those unnatural eyes hold me at a standstill. There is something in those obsidian hues that say more than she'll ever reveal.

But a sharp nod from me has her turning to face the bed. The zip of her hoody coming off sounds the air. I walk the few steps to her dresser next to the door, and turn the chair to face the bed.

My eyes never leave her as she removes her denims, her naked ass staring at me.

There is no hesitance, no innocence left in her to care for her lack of clothes.

The girl is thin as a beggar should be. She pulls down the covers still stark naked then un twists her long hair until it flows down her back.

I can see the promise of her. But I don't linger on her body any longer.

I grab a t-shirt from the dresser and throw it at her.

It's Venus's and she slips it on before hopping under the covers.

It's minutes later her breathing changes. The dim ceiling lights show me her form. The long breaths she takes means she's sleeping.

I should leave now.

But my legs refuse me.

It's a few hours later, I'm on the carpeted floor, pillow under my head. My ears are always aware, awake more so when I'm sober. Sleep doesn't come easy, it never does. The promise of a hot morning lighting up the room.

The sound of choking gets me up on my feet.

What I see before me makes even an emotionless sadist like me flinch in horror.

She's choking on something in her mouth and it doesn't take a genius to figure out what she's dreaming about. Her hands are clawing her neck, her legs splayed open.

But what got me, what really fucking gets me even now, is that her stomach's visible, showing the burn marks over her torso.

My steps are silent as not to wake her just yet.

I need to get closer.

I'm stopped short when Beggar gets up, her eyes wide and alert, her skin misted in a light sheen of sweat.

She sees me then seems to remember where she is.

There are no tears in her depths, no regrets, or emotion besides the labored breathing and red lacerations she made around her neck and chest.

"You have permission to touch me, only you."

I can tell by her dead stare and words, that this is something important, she doesn't just give people rights to touch her.

I give her a sharp nod in response.

For the first time I'm speechless. Tongue tied.

And maybe just maybe not as emotionless as I thought.

X

I have a room. An actual room with a shower inside and my own toilet. Killer explained to me that I'd have to clean it up myself, but it's mine to decorate as I want.

No one has ever done anything for me, and this entire experience since I got here so far is so unreal, I wait for the show to end, for the players to stop acting and reveal their trueselves.

I wasn't really sure how to feel about it last night when Killer opened the room. A bed big enough for two filled the center and a white dresser with a mirror attached to it took the left side next to the bedroom door.

The one side of 'my room' has a window with two white wardrobes on either side. There's a bathroom behind a white door directly opposite the blue linen covered bed that's all mine.

Small dim lights glowed from the white ceiling. It was too much that I just stood staring. I never stayed in anything half as clean. Half as nice.

When he made to leave, I stopped him, asked him to stay while I fell off to sleep. With the devil in the room I thought he'll keep the dreams away.

Killer is dangerous and a killer, maybe. But he isn't the true evil.

He intimidated me.

Messed with my mind.

But this morning I watched how he cared for Chadley when she cut her hand slicing a pineapple.

When I woke up from a nightmare, he wasn't touching me, wasn't comforting me. He knew I didn't like to be touched and I didn't have to tell him.

Killer respected my wishes and for that I granted him permission to touch me. Apart of me knows he won't do it unless it is necessary.

This morning I was woken up by a guy with blonde shoulder length hair and light blue eyes. Killer was gone. My door ajar.

My legs were off the bed in seconds. I paused to take in this man. He was smaller built than the others. Dressed in a grey track pants and loose white tee. I saw him with us in Washington, wearing a bandana over his head. He was one of the two guys who were at the club.

"I'm Spade, nice to see you well rested."

"Yeah."

He shoved a pack of clothes in my chest and a pair of tennis shoes next. He was careful not to touch me or get too close.

"You're on kitchen duty. Move your ass, you got 10 minutes to be downstairs or I'm coming back up." He was gone.

It was half that time before I was downstairs.

A new day, a new start.

I'm mopping the floor to Dorothy - raise hell. The flap door to the kitchen shoves my weightless thoughts out. I spin around, mop in hand and squint my eyes to the group of females shuffling in the kitchen.

Venus is the one in front. Falon to her right wearing a white shorts and matching tank top. Damn she's tiny.

"How ya doing Beggar?" Venus asks in an over cheerily voice.

I can admit that I'm a bit startled.

These women haven't been overly welcoming to my arrival.

"Okay. Wassup?" I reply, my defense unbidden.

Falon steps forward, the red headed girl is sexy as well as confident.

"I wanted to thank you for saving me. And thought we might go out, shopping and dancing, my treat. What do you say Beggar?"

I stare at her, I'm a bit stunned.

Well speechless, yeah, that's it.

She wants to take me shopping and dancing. I glance at the other girls. Chadley, with her bug blue eyes, small pesky nose and round face stares at me in encouragement.

Weird.

Her purple hair is wicked though.

Venus got a small smirk on her lips, no doubt she's in charge.

I can see it by her stance and the way Wisp stands behind her, shooting me daggers but quickly diverts her gaze when Venus turns around to face her.

The entire scene makes me wanna laugh. I'm in one of these girl's old clothes. Mop in hand, hoody on.

They are all dressed, with make-up and shit, all girly, lots of hips and tits on display.

The kitchen that was smelling thick of disinfectant minutes ago is now mixed with various smells of feminine perfumes.

They sure as shit make an effort.

"Yeah, okay. When's this happening?" My vibe is relaxed, but inside I'm laughing.

It's clear to me that if the girls weren't forced by Venus, they wouldn't have asked me shit.

Falon already thanked me yesterday.

She doesn't seem like the type to dwell on much and has enough to worry about with a sick father than me.

And Wisp thinks I stole her man, but we both know that shit ain't true. And Chadley, well she just doesn't seem like she really considered me actually a part of the house.

I don't blame her.

I like the invisibility.

The other girl Jade is gone, she left the minute we got back.

Venus however did share a few words but she wasn't sending me invitations to become pals and shit in the future.

Which means, the orders came from higher up. Maybe I should be hurt by this, but fuck, they offering me a night out and shopping.

They know I'm broke so I won't be paying for shit.

When you on the streets you learn when to fight your battles and when to deal your hand.

But mostly you learn when to take the little moments you get to live and triple it into months of the best memories you'll ever have.

"Saturday after your shift, so around 5-ish. And before I forget, your training finishes at 3 today," Venus shares, "Consider it your one and only boon."

I stare at Venus, not sure I'm hearing correct,

"Training?"

She smiles, "Yes, training. You officially a Prospect. And as a Prospect, you have to undergo the training program. As well as a part time job which starts Saturday."

My gaze darts to Wisp who's face looks stoic.

"Do I get paid?"

"Yeah, you get an allowance as all the Prospects. And a monthly salary for working. But you only start earning pay next month."

When my face cracks in a smile, I feel my cheeks stretching taut.

"We'll see you later Beggar. Oh, and Chadley will loan you something to wear," Falon says, while the others file out.

I nod, and she opens her mouth to say something else but catches herself and walks out.

All too soon, I'm mopping the light grey kitchen tiles, that Killer insists are white.

My thoughts are on how much I'm going to get paid.

And what the hell does Venus mean by training? I open the back door and lift the bucket up.

I practically jump out of my skin when a deep throat clears behind me.

The bucket of dirty water falls on the step and the grass as I spin around and find myself staring at the one man I don't want to see, Zero.

"Are you just going to stand there or help me out."

It's then I notice he's holding grocery bags in both hands and a pack of beer under his arm.

His face cracks at what I think is a partial smile.

He seems so relaxed today apart from the leather pants and black t-shirt of course.

It's almost like he was... My mind screams to shut the thought down and my eyes widen as I stumble back.

Invisible fingers start chocking me.

The mop drops from my hand as I lift my arms to fend off my attacker.

"Don't you dare." Zero screams but this time I don't listen to his command as I lose my footing, falling on the wet tiled floor.

I pull the invisible fingers constricting my air supply, my nails clawing my already bruised neck, my eyes bulging.

It's too bad that it feels so real, that I can't tell present from past.

My scream as I feel hands bind my own on top of my head is the last memory I have before I fade.

"Wake up, Beauty." Zero's imposing voice says to me.

"No." I reply in a wince, the rawness of my throat informing me that I had an 'episode'. It's what a stripper called it when I flipped in front of her.

"Come on, you gotta drink some water, you've been out like a light for two hours."

He actually sounds like he cares, concerned, ha.

"My names Beggar." I clear my throat, my eyes still not open.

He laughs softly.

"No, it's not, and as long as you refuse to tell me your name, I'm gonna call you Beauty. It's suiting don'tcha think?" He drawls in a thick Texan accent.

I open one eye and instantly regret it.

He's practically leaning over me and the big smile on his face is too much for me.

"No, I don't think. Could you sit there." I point to the bottom of my bed. He frowns and has a fucking nerve to look offended, as if.

"Why? Is my handsome face too much for you?"

I open both my eyes at the question.

"Handsome?" I snort and grimace when my throat pains.

"Scary, is more like it."

He laughs as he leans closer.

My eyes grow wider, "What are you doing?" I hiss, "I don't like to be touched, don't you know."

"I carried you upstairs and I can assure you that you liked it, don't you know."

I scramble into a sitting position, knees to my chest, hair falling over my face, hands on my toes. Head to my knees but it doesn't touch, it mustn't.

"You have no reason to be scared of me Beauty. You know I would never hurt you. Someone else hurt you, not me. You wanna talk about it? Tell me who hurt you." His tone drops, cajoling, like a professional predator leering its prey into servitude.

I watch his face from the gaps of my hair. He rakes his fingers through his hair, before the same fingers goes to play with the 3-inch scar under his eye.

"Do I?" I dry whisper as my head tilts to get a better glimpse at him through the small gap in my hair.

"Yes! Deep down you know. Drink your water Beauty, lunch is in twenty."

"I'm not ready to share," I say.

He stares really hard at me, like he can see me but it's not possible because I'm covered right?

"You already have Beauty, and soon I'll know all your secrets."

Zero gets up and walks to the door.

I barely turn my head to watch him, seeing if he'll turn.

He doesn't.

I'm not sure what I feel when he closes the door. I just know it is dangerous, very dangerous.

The pudding next to my bed in line with the water just reinforces what I already know, dread, him being right.

XI

I 'm standing in the barn. It's a wooden shed that's as big as a house with high hooks hanging from the ceiling, well what's left of the ceiling.

Lots of dry grass stacked up in high piles fill the place, which is for the horses. Call me dumb but I didn't know horses ate grass.

On the corner is a long table pushed against the wooden wall with various tools lined up on the top.

After lunch, Storm told me to walk to the barn and wait for one of them to meet me here and give me a run-down of the program and training I'll be doing.

The door to the barn is open and my feet are itching to just go outside. But Killer told me during lunch that the first rule about being a Prospect of The Satan Sniper's MC is- listen to your instructors.

And I have for twenty minutes.

That's how long I'm waiting under the hot Southern sky. The barn got half the roof missing, the part that doesn't have grass under it, the only place I can stand.

The boisterous laughter from outside has me going to see who it is, I've always been a nosey body. Living with a bunch of bikers isn't going to change that.

The man walking toward me has my insides boiling. My feet want to move, and get as far away from this man as I can, but knowing that, I still can't look away.

He didn't say a word to anyone about my episode earlier. In-fact he acted as if he didn't even speak to me, and as much as I want to hate the biker, he is making it hard to.

Zero's walking toward me with his phone in one hand. He's darker, scarier than he was this morning. His body is encompassed in a thick dull leather pants.

The bulk I see between his legs is hard to miss, poor Falon. I divert my eyes to the two silver chains hanging off the one side of his pants while telling myself he has a girlfriend and I'm not attracted to men. I avoid them, that is what's best.

The same black tee he wore this morning stretches around his arms and chest, loose around his waist.

He must wear a XXL in his tees. His body I know from feeling it is completely ripped. No fat is creeping its way on him anytime soon.

My eyes wander up his chiseled body and I cringe when I look at him, he's staring right back at me, and that laugh I heard a few seconds ago is completely gone, so is the phone from his hand.

His steps approach me and this is about the time I'm supposed to get red in the cheeks or lower my gaze. Well, some girly thing like that.

And maybe if my name was Falon I would but it ain't. So, I stare the fucker in his face, my black eyes no doubt dead.

Zero is intimidating on a good day, and he's instilled his fear in me but he has also informed me that he wouldn't hurt me.

I'm sure he wouldn't physically hurt me and I don't think about the other ways he could hurt me.

Truth is, I'm so fucked up that unless I'm dealing with my monster or my sixth sense is screaming at me to cower I ain't doing it.

There's danger coming off Zero but no anger, maybe disgust or wariness, but there's nothing telling me he's going to slaughter me, and feed me to his dogs.

It's confusing to why I wanna hide from him, run from him, but can't seem to keep my eyes off of him.

"Hey."

He greets me, stopping just a few steps into the barn, a few feet closer to me.

"Hi, yourself," I croak, 'cause my throat still hurts from the screaming

"Ah, I..I'm...I'm just waiting for Storm."

He arches his thick brow, his green eyes a shade lighter under the natural outside light, whilst his skin has adopted a deep golden tan.

"Storm ha," he rubs his index finger on his scar under his eye.

"Hate to break it to you but you've been waiting for me, and well done."

"What did I do?"

He drops his hand and slides it into his pocket, his features change. I'd say he's more relaxed.

"You passed rule number one."

Regardless of the mean big scary biker my face cracks and I'm smiling. My guess was correct, I knew this was a test but only because of Killer's warning. I'm going to have to thank him.

"It's the first time I'm seeing you smile so big."

I shrug, "It's the second time today."

He stiffens, but I don't pay it any mind,

"You count how many times you smile?"

"When you live on the streets you count everything, smiling is just one of the good things," I answer him truthfully.

"I'm a beggar, I'm not an alien Zero."

People forget that we can laugh, talk, listen, cry. Many people pass us in fancy cars on the street and most will put the window up, or drive faster.

Some think, 'why don't they go work, get a job.'

It's easy to think that when you going home to a hot meal and warm bed.

Some of us just can't. Some of us are hiding, running, living in fear. Others are searching for the easy way out, and quick buck, or a habit to support.

A few just don't know any other way, they don't want the change.

"It's easy to judge when you outside looking in," I tell him.

What it's not easy to do is see the truth.

The people on the street all have stories, theirs are just much worse than others.

And I say this because regardless of what people think, having that extra nest of cash or a steady job makes all the difference when faced with horror.

Money is a false sense of comfort, but comfort it is.

I get a sharp nod in response, his green gaze steady as he stares right into me.

"Let's get out of here, then we can talk about the program."

His words send a garble of unwanted heat to my core at the thought of being close to him.

I need to get away from him, I need to get far away from Zero.

My eyes widen a fraction, it's the one thing I still do, the small thread of my humanity,

"I didn't know we gotta leave."

"We ain't gotta do anything besides what I say Beauty."

His head tilts, like he's hoping for me to retort, maybe even wants it.

I frown and wipe my hands on my borrowed jeans.

"Are you always so bossy. My names Beggar," I say in a small whisper. My hands are so sweaty all of a sudden.

"Are you always so secretive? You not really expecting me to call you Beggar, now are you?"

He takes a step closer to me, and I want to step back, but I know if I'm not careful I'll find myself backed against a corner, and I'm not a girl who wants to be cornered by a predator.

So, I do the only thing I can, I swallow, and answer truthfully,

"You more than others."

He closes the space between us in seconds. My heart is drumming so fast even he can see the quick rise and fall of my chest. I expect him to grab me, shake me, or something involving rough contact.

Zero does neither.

My neck rises so I'm face to face with the man I fear, the man with the scar under his left eye. The one man who controls my demons with just a word, a man who has power over me. A stranger that makes me feel things I've never wanted to feel, never thought I could. A man who's called Zero.

He bends his head down, to my right side of my neck.

I go to take that step back. I tried not too but I see the error of my ways. I should know that lambs never wait for the wolf.

"Don't." His sharp demand has me staying just there.

I close my eyes and tilt my head, waiting to see what he'll do, what he'll take.

The intake of breath on my neck is not what I expect, nor is the knot in my stomach from the action.

I open my eyes and find he's taken a step back, his features hard, angry almost.

The feelings I have turn sour. He isn't trying to capture my scent or some corny fucked up shit like that. The asshole was checking to see if I'm still smelling.

The thought hardens me, and it's a shit thing to do but fuck it. I walk past him, sniff him and spit on the ground before I storm away.

Zero's feet are behind me, but he isn't speeding up, just keeping pace.

I untangle my hoody from around my waist and slip my arms into it. And I'm sure as the sun is hot, I'm going to fry, but I don't give a dime.

I wanna hide, I just want to be invisible.

XII

She's staring out the window. That fucking hoody blocking her face. I'm going to burn that fucking piece of clothing, it's driving me crazy. I can't see her.

I can't fucking tell if she's upset or what.

We were walking toward my bike when I saw Falon standing on the porch outside. It's like she was waiting to see what I was going to do, and if I'm being honest, I was putting Beggar's ass on the back of my bike.

It was what I wanted, it just felt normal. Beggar was walking in front of me and that's where she was headed too.

One glimpse at Falon's hurt face had me turning around and going to my Jeep instead. My words were clipped when I told Beggar to get her ass in the car.

The hood covering her face served as a barrier between us even as she did what I asked and I hated that something I did caused that.

I felt her stiffen when we jumped in the cage.

I'm not even sure why I care. These feelings are driving me up the wall.

I don't wanna feel this shit. I've been conditioned not to feel, not to care. But this girl, this girl just conjures up something in me and I fucking hate her for it.

Beggar felt something earlier in the barn. Her body was begging me for everything and more.

I'm a man. It's why I got so close to her, why I inhaled her airy scent, no other reason.

She pretends she's all anti-men but It's an act, it has to be. No one has done that to me, no woman has ever made me want her beyond reasoning. That was seduction she did in there, a pure golden temptress.

Her skin didn't flush as she tilted her neck in that way and lowered her eyes, her lips parting.

I adjust my position on the seat. My cock is almost fully erect by that image.

I glance at her from the corner of my eyes. Her face is glued to the window and I know the views for shit.

Something happened in the Barn. The temptress became a guarded soul but only after she sniffed me, spat on the ground and stormed out.

My feet and pride had me turning and going after her. I've never chased after a woman besides Falon and for good reason. Yet, I sure as shit wanted to know what happened in there, even if I was just pissed that she was the one unaffected and I was the one with blue balls.

After one look at that ass in those jeans my anger was forgotten. The girl is sure as shit thin, but damn if she doesn't have an ass. And I was watching it move as she walked, like a man possessed.

No hesitance in her movements, no extra sway in those hips. Nothing. She was walking naturally but that ass.

I don't have to wonder if she knows how fucking sexy her ass is when she's marching.

It has a slight jiggle, flesh to grab, unlike the rest of her body.

If she knew, there's no way she would be living on the street.

Some man would be a lucky bastard one day, that's for damn sure.

Killers face flashes in my mind just out of nowhere.

I chance another look at her.

A million questions and scenarios come to mind. But there are three questions screaming in my head louder than the others.

Could Beggar want Killer?

Need him?

Is she really submissive?

Killer turned Venus down this morning to spend his time playing watch dog for Beggar. When Spade shared that shit with me this morning, I was speechless.

Killer's an emotionless bastard most of the time and that's on his good days. He has never turned down sex for anyone.

The thought of the two of them together has me squeezing the steering wheel tighter.

Keep it together.

This isn't good.

My jaw clenches and though my vision never fades I know I'm going to break the steering wheel.

I can feel the strain my fingers are putting on the car part, it's almost there, at breaking point.

Years of training as a hunter in the special ops taught me the signs of knowing when I'm losing it.

And there's no doubt in my mind that my rational thoughts are slipping away.

This is really not good. We're in the middle of the freeway.

I know not to blame myself. I never know what's going to trigger me losing my shit.

I never know what's going to turn me into the cold heartless hunter I'm trained to be.

I just know I need to keep Beggar safe, keep her safe from me.

I go into auto pilot.

The first thing I do is assess my situation.

If I stop the cage, I'm going to have Beggar on the trunk of it with her legs splayed open.

Me, balls deep inside her snatch and I'm not going to be able to stop for hours. She isn't going to be safe.

No, not safe at all.

If I talk to her first then she's going to win and that might just end in the same way, me in between those thighs.

Shaking my head, I try to clear my thoughts.

There isn't many options left.

After a minute I do the only other thing I can do, I put my foot on the accelerator needing to feel in control.

I can keep her safe, I'm in control. I repeat the mantra silently.

The window goes down and I increase the volume of the song,

'Kick it in the sticks' by Brentley Gilbert. *How fucking fetching.*

She doesn't make a sound or say a word and that just pisses me off more. She's okay with not talking to me. Why the fuck does it piss me off?

I don't like it.

She should want to say something.

Ask me something.

"You don't have to yell, and put that damn song softer." She snaps.

It takes me a minute to register I said it out loud.

"Then why are you so fucking quiet, you talk to Killer and Storm." The accusatory tone of my voice is stark. But I'm beyond caring at this moment.

I focus on the road, drop the music from the buttons on the steering wheel but not the speed. All the while my body is waging a war within itself.

"Storm is easy to talk to and Killer is just, persistent." She's so honest.

But I also know she can be a good liar. All homeless people are.

"And me?" I take my eyes off the empty road to glance at her. Her face is still facing the Window.

"Not easy to talk to," She rasps dryly in her deep baritone like it's so obvious.

I smirk and my body starts to calm itself down but I stay silent as I make the turn into the gravel road and park by the entrance of the park.

"I'm not that bad, ask me something." My eyes steady on her hooded face that is still facing the open window.

"I don't think that's a good idea."

"Ask me!" I snap.

"Stop shouting at me like I'm an imbecile. I don't wanna ask you any question. I don't wanna know anything about you."

"Why not?"

She's quiet seeming to consider her answer.

"You keep bossing me around to do what you want when you want but then you treat me like a plague. It's clear you don't want me here."

The retort is on my lips, but she sighs shaking her hooded head.

"I get it. I'm a filthy beggar from the streets, a dirt-poor shady female that won't tell you her name, living with your people. It's bound to cause problems Zero. But I'm no threat to your club, and me keeping my shit private is keeping my promise." Her deep dry voice never wavers or rises and she never drops her hood.

I start to say something, I'm not even certain what, I just know those words don't gel well with me.

My phone flashes with Falon's name interrupting me. I disconnect the call and switch my phone off.

I fling it on the dashboard and rake my hands into my hair before my finger slides across the scar under my eye.

My scar is a reminder to never trust easily, never let my guard down long enough for anyone besides the hand full of people I trust to see past the walls I've created.

The silence in the car would be deafening if not for my harsh breathing.

The park is dead this time of day, it's why I picked it to explain stuff to Beggar.

"You ain't planning on leaving me here are you."

My hand is on the door and my entire body stiffens when she asks me that.

Not only does she think that I consider her a filthy beggar but she thinks I'm an asshole that will chuck a female in a foreign place to fend for herself.

It's the second time I've heard that vulnerable tinge in her voice and it fucking guts me until I have this sick knot twisting in my stomach, because I know it's coming from a strong woman who was broken beyond compare.

I turn to look at her, and I lose my thoughts, I lose my hearing, my feeling, everything except my eyes.

Her hood is down and her black guarded eyes are staring directly at me.

Something starts to take hold of me, something otherworldly and unexplainable pushing me to protect this girl, to know her, see her, own her, save her.

I can't take my eyes off her; I know that's exactly what I should do.

This is wrong, she's a beggar and I'm a taken man. But a small voice whisper, mine.

"I'll never leave you."

The sharp intake of her breath and widened eyes brings me back to my senses and what I said.

I clear my throat.

"I'm the Enforcer and you're one of us. As a member of The Satan Snipers you have the club's protection like everyone else."

The relief in her shoulders is a good reminder of how she became one of us and why I should stay away from her, if not physically then mentally.

I just need to keep reminding myself that and pray I make it through this with my rational thoughts intact.

After all, I am the fucking Enforcer of the club.

Beggar is still a girl full of secrets and we know nothing about her but what she shared. She could be a hired spy, just playing the part well.

I need to keep my head straight.

When we get back to the club, I got a woman to claim, and her name sure as shit ain't Beggar.

XIII

I t's Friday, and five days since my training started. I've been focusing mostly on shooting and physical training.

The shooting is going great. Killer said I'm a natural. No surprise there. The physical part, well that just sucks ass. My stamina is good but my strength is for shit.

Venus suggested a high carb diet, so for the past three days my eating habits have increased to six meals a day. Not sure what good that's going to do, but what do I know.

Killer and Zero are my primary instructors. That's what I was told by Zero the day he explained shit to me anyway but Killer is more invested which is fine by me.

Zero is, well I'm not sure what he is but I'm just going to say he is generous, and his generosity spreads in the form of 'allowing' as Spade calls it; the others namely, Spade, Snake, Knight and Storm to train me in his place.

Ofcourse that is unless Rounder makes an appearance then he's there. Moody and full of shit, but he is there.

My close combat training has been put on hold until I become 'comfortable' in my own skin. Spade taught me the first day. He's the best in close combat, which I found as a surprise. I'm pretty sure he's the smallest built guy in the club.

It all was going great.

I was learning different ways of blocking punches until he touched me, it was a slight touch on my upper arm. I busted his nose; it was a mistake and I told him so. I also warned him not to touch me again.

The good thing was that he finished the lesson, in return I helped him strap his nose. I also explained to Spade that I didn't mind touching a man, I just minded a man touching me.

On the second day of combat, Killer arrived. I know I said he could touch me and we were good with the arm touches and leg stuff but then his hand touched my stomach.

He was just getting up from the carpet. My legs instinctively kicked out and I kneed him in the manhood.

Not my favorite moment. He said he was okay but I couldn't hear much with all his gobbling.

We didn't finish the lesson but I did get him ice for his manhood.

Then Zero showed up yesterday being his broody asshole self.

I haven't spoken to him much since that day in the park, unless his barking orders was considered 'talking.'

He just switched off that day in the park. I thought by saying what I said I was giving him an out. I think a piece of me thought that he'd be nicer.

His body was like stone when he explained the program to me in auto mode, and that was that.

I tried to pretend I didn't notice his episode in the monster vehicle he calls a cage and I know I succeeded so I knew it was me.

That day in the park was one of the longest hours of my life.

After that, the man started behaving similar to Texas and Killer, but where Killer and Texas didn't know any better and did it to everyone. Zero just had a cold indifference to me.

At least his words were few to none in the five days since. At first, I admit that I was a tiny bit sad by that and I mean very tiny.

The girls were making an effort to be civil and the men were taking time explaining stuff to me.

Zero was the only one who made me feel unwelcome. The only one who threatened my chance at a new start.

It didn't do good things for my mind.

So, when he came in the training room on the top floor, I told him I didn't think it was a good idea he trained me and that I preferred Killer and Spade.

I was more comfortable around them. He just gave me a tight-lipped smile and proceeded with the lesson like I hadn't said shit.

Most of the lesson I was surprised when he didn't touch me, and that made me feel better. But all good things had to blah blah.

We were going over side and front punches when he barked at me to do push-ups.

I didn't want to inform him that Spade told me that my arms were too skinny and I wouldn't be able to hold my body weight on it without a month of lifting weights.

The guy seemed to hate the sight of me. It was obvious Zero didn't want to be stuck training me and I didn't know what else to do.

I'd given him many outs.

What more could I do?

I proceeded, and weren't surprised when I couldn't get back up. Zero chose that moment to put his hand under my torso to lift me.

I thrashed and he snapped, yelling at me to stop but didn't move his hand.

I tried hitting him, I tried turning but the asshole put his knee on my back and kept me on the ground.

My body went into shock and my monster came creeping by.

It was hours later I found myself in bed with a sleeping Killer next to me.

Since the first night Killer and I had agreed to share the bed. We had a silent agreement of no touching and he didn't betray our nonverbal agreement so I went back to sleep.

This morning I woke up, went straight downstairs to put the coffee on and start cleaning the kitchen. Which is my assigned house chore for the week as we all have to do household chores, no matter your rank.

"You live here, you eat here, you sleep here, then you damn as sure clean here." That's how Rounder explained it to me. I wouldn't mind if I had to clean the entire house by myself.

I was just glad I had a place to sleep and a meal to eat.

I was on my hands and knees, using the scrubbing brush on the floor cleaning up the dried dough off the tiles. Brent Eldredge - Don't ya was blaring from the lounge area.

I might've lived on the street of Washington but I knew music.

I used to spend hours in the music shop a block from Lazers just listening to tracks.

The lady that works there didn't mind, she even gave me old food a few times.

Pity I'm so far away now.

The sound of someone's footsteps coming into the kitchen had me up from the floor to greet whoever it was.

I grimaced at the sight before me and the words died in my mouth.

Zero's green eyes glared from across the space.

Cringing at the sight of his jaw that had a purple and blue bruise darkening by the minute as it swelled up on the right side of his face.

He dropped his menacing stare and sauntered closer to the coffee pot trying to hide the tiny limp. It would've worked if I hadn't caught the grimace and soft groan.

I knew who did that to him. Yeah, I knew exactly who because this morning Killer's knuckles were red.

I asked him what happened and he said something just kept falling into his fist.

We both laughed but seeing the 'something' I felt bad.

It was my fault. They shouldn't have been fighting because of me.

That thought was what led me to here and now. It's the sole reason how I found myself in Zero's room.

He's laying down on his black duvet. I got an ice pack to his jaw and he just asked me to put ointment on his back.

In the kitchen I apologized and expected something, well I wasn't sure what I expected, but the apology from him wasn't it.

I softened at that. No one has ever apologized to me. So, I offered to put ice on his bruises.

Funny thing what a week with a group of bikers can teach you. Ice packs, heat rub and iceman were the norm of the day around here.

I was waiting for the sharp no to come from Zero's mouth and had already gotten back on the ground to continue with the floors.

Zero stunned me when his answer was "follow me."

And I did, right upstairs into his monstrosity of a room, with a mini fridge, sitting area and bathroom big enough for six.

He got the ice pack from his freezer and handed it to me before he threw himself on his bed fit for a king and patted the space next to him.

Now here we are, his expectant gaze letting me know he is serious.

The Enforcer of The Satan Snipers wants me to put ointment on his back.

"I... I...ah." I swallow and clear my throat, "I don't think that's something I should, you should, ah."

"What? I should, you should? You not making any sense Beauty. I've helped you when you needed it, carrying a dead weight girl up thirty steps aren't easy and I said please."

The innocent curious expression riddling his face doesn't belong on him. It's not right, but does the trick when he uses that word.

My eyes become saucers at that word and I squirm.

This is my cue to leave this room.

He can see the wheels in my head spinning no doubt. My eyes dart to the door more times than I'll ever admit.

I'm not chicken. I swear I'm not.

The Enforcer finds my fright to flight funny. His body shakes the bed from silent laughter.

Decision made I drop the icepack next to his pillow and stand up.

I hate being a laughing stock. It's the one thing I haven't gotten immune to no matter how many times it has happened.

"Don't you wanna know what's so funny?"

"No, I really don't. I'll go call Falon." I turn around toward the white door that's looking more appealing by the second.

"No." His harsh voice barks through the walls it's so loud.

I turn around and glare at him but my anger falls flat when I see him struggling to turn on his stomach.

"I can do this, it's just ointment." I say aloud, but it's for myself not him.

Just ointment on his back and then I'm done. A MAN'S back. I close my eyes; *I can do this.*

"Beauty come on." That word again. Why is he using that word?

I walk toward his bed, closer to him and stop.

"Call me Beggar."

"No."

I turn my attention to him which was seconds ago on the plush grey carpet.

Zero might be in pain, but I can see it in his hard eyes, that scar creasing under his left eye that he isn't going to call me Beggar.

He's an asshole.

I stand there not sure what to do.

Sighing, he loses some of the harshness.

"If you want me to call you something else tell me your name."

I tread the distance closer to him, nudging him so he lays on his stomach.

"My name is Beggar. Who I was isn't important."

We both quieten as I lift his white tee up.

The scars on his back are the first thing I notice. Seeing him like this feels too intimate. A shudder runs up my back.

I lift the fabric higher; the beginnings of a tattoo start to show.

My fingers mistakenly graze a stab wound and he shivers at the touch.

"You need to lift up." I murmur clearing my throat.

He hisses when he lifts his body up and I manage to get his t-shirt all the way to his shoulders until his entire back is on display.

He has multiple scars. Some from gunshots, some from knife fights, and others from whips.

The tattoo covers most of them.

My hands itch to touch his imperfections. They are the scars of his life, what shaped him into the man he is, the one he'll become.

It's all part of life.

My mother always said that the choices we make determine who we become.

I never made bright choices, but they were the choices I made, and I lived with them.

I didn't come out on the top, but I keep breathing, keep putting one step in front of the other because I'm a survivor.

I, like Zero wear my scars on the outside and inside.

It takes me a second but I see it.

This man is a lot like me.

A fighter.

The thought makes me smile.

never thought I'll compare myself to someone, least of all a man.

These feeling are foreign to me.

The male population has always been a means to an end.

The worse of the bunch.

I know that there are some men who are great, but I haven't had the luck to meet any.

But luck granted me a reprieve from bad fortune the day I saved Falon's life.

These men of The Satan Snipers are not nice but they are kind.

And maybe Zero doesn't like me, maybe he does secretly want me gone, but he is no monster.

I focus on his marred flesh. I find it harder to inhale the air in the room as it thickens. Maybe it's getting hotter I'm not sure.

I hope I'm not getting a cold.

My attention is on Zero's many back muscles as they ripple and flex under my scrutiny.

Can he feel my eyes on his skin?

I admire the tattoo taking up most of his back, it's similar to Storms.

It's a pair of evil snake eyes in red, with a green and yellow snake wrapped around the pistol facing the red eyes of the evil snake. The words The Satan Sniper's Motorcycle Club are written under the pistol.

But what has me at a standstill is the shading that's done around the entire picture, it's a light shading but unmistakable.

It's wings, Angel wings.

I don't say anything.

I want to but I'm tongue tied. I scan his back and stop at the blue bruises around his sides.

Killer did a number on him and I'm not sure how to feel about that.

I mimic his earlier expression and sigh as I pick up the ointment off the nightstand.

I pour the cold gel straight on his back.

He doesn't move a muscle when it drops in the center of his indented spine.

Taking a deep breath, I rub my hands together then place them on his hot skin.

My fingers glide to the side of his hardened flesh where the bruises are. Up and down I rub the wounded flesh.

The smell of the menthol rub fills the air and I pour more gel and get bolder.

My fingers start to go over his battle scars, because that's what they are.

Zero is a soldier,

a hero.

His healed wounds are a myriad of memories, a reminder of what he endured for his country, for millions of people.

My scars are for one, just one.

My fingers dig in when I feel a knot on his lower spine.

I close my hand into a tight fist then work his muscles with my knuckles losing myself in the process.

My mother taught me how to massage.

She was good at it, and insisted I learnt at least one thing from her.

Time goes and my hands are red from over usage.

It could be an hour or more I'm not sure.

I'm just lost in the feel of his now heated skin under my fingers and knuckles and the human contact I've allowed myself.

I don't think of anything but my knuckles digging in this man's flesh.

I should've paid more attention. The stiff posture of his shoulders, the heat coming from his skin. I should've understood the charge in the air but I didn't.

My hands are on his back, I'm putting my all into this massage.

His body spins so fast I have no time to react before I find myself under him.

The bed barely bounces, then he's looming over me, his one hand has my wrist in an unyielding grip.

His eyes are filled with carnality.

His nostrils flare like a raging bull and I gulp as my heart jackhammers inside my chest. My eyes like saucers.

I'm a deer trapped under a starved beast. His thick thighs wedge in between my thin ones, showing me his power over me.

He wants me to understand it, to know without a doubt that when it comes to him, I'm defenseless.

He leaves me no second to protest or act out, he just bends down and his mouth is over mine.

I've kissed three guys my whole life and that was when I was barely sixteen. And this is nothing like that.

There's no hesitance or uncertainty that I wouldn't want it.

No, Zero's tongue is demanding for entry.

His lips are firm, hard and taste like beer. I open my mouth to, I don't know, but he takes that as an in, and then I'm lost in a haze.

I kiss him back, my lips moving in-sync to his, a fast-paced dance.

We kissing, actually kissing I tell myself.

It's angry and hard, his tongue is sucking on mine that it's so close to painful.

Zero is not just kissing me he's consuming me, dominating me.

I feel it right in the center of my legs.

His chest comes down firmly on my own, crushing me, but it's so fucking amazing that for the first time in years, I just don't care.

My lips are stinging.

Zero does something with his tongue that I feel right in my toes.

It is causing a throaty sound to rip from my torturous throat. That makes him more frenzy and he rotates his hips so his cock is grinding against my denim covered pussy, all while he's tongue fucking my mouth.

Because that's exactly what he's doing. He is fucking my mouth hard like a man possessed.

His fingers are still serving as a restraint locked around my wrists.

His other hand slides under my ass, lifting me up and pulling me harder into him, at the same time he rocks his hips against me.

There is no space between us as his body encompasses mine.

Emotions claw its way in me and I lose myself in him. I start mimicking his movements in the opposite direction.

There's nothing sexy about this, there's nothing soft and sweet about this either.

I'm not sure how long we kiss. I'm not sure how we doing it, or why I'm not freaking out.

I'm just in this moment as he lights my body into a fast burning fire.

His hand leaves my wrist and mine instantly fly to his ass, bringing him closer to me, squeezing his tight flesh as my legs lock around his hips, wanting more, something deeper.

His free hand joins the one under my ass and I have no choice but to lift my hands and dig my fingers into his shoulders.

He hisses in my mouth and his movements get faster and harder, our breathing and sound of our rough humping fills the menthol scented air.

His right-hand slips under my back.

Zero's hands are huge and my nerves spike at the same time my core tightens when his fingers fan out to the full expand of my lower back before he lifts me partially off the bed.

I arch closer to him, my lips burning from the kiss of death he's still bestowing upon me. It's almost like he's afraid to let up, afraid to stop.

Zero's fingers gather up my blue t-shirt, while the length of his hardness rubs against my wet covered pussy.

The touch of his fingers against my naked skin is almost enough to blow my mind.

His rough fingers dig into my flesh and makes their way to my stomach.

It's like throwing me in the Northern river as the cold hard reality crashes into me in the seconds that tick on by.

I stiffen as my memories fight for front seat, fight to steal this away, like it has stolen in the past. Burning iron assaults my nose.

No, please, No.

I stop the kiss and turn my head, my battle with my demons waging on me.

But Zero is lost in the moment, he licks my neck, sucking on the pulsing vein.

And it takes everything to let go of this moment without shattering this reprieve.

The first humanly contact I had freely given since I fell prey to a beautiful monster.

"I'm sorry, I..I..cant." My voice breaks as I stammer for syllables.

My breathing is labored as I try to push Zero off me.

He freezes, his mouth glistening and partly red from my macerations.

I watch and wait in silence. His green gaze takes in my face, which I'm sure is dead. That's how I have to be.

That's how I need to feel to survive my demons, my monster.

I watch in silence as his own rough features glimmer with his inner emotions, realization, regret, disgust, disbelief, and finally coldness, a coldness I've come to understand this week for what it truly is.

A coldness of a deadly killer, a coldness of a *sniper*.

"Leave then. Run away, Get. The. Fuck. Out." He grinds the words between his clenched teeth.

I don't have to be asked again as I practically stumble off his bed.

I'm not sure how, but I make it to the door.

My hand on the knob.

"I can't believe I thought... I..you know what you nothing but a fucking beggar."

I swallow at his brutal words, but remain silent.

Waiting for him to say the rest, to plunge the knife he wishes to twist into my heart, my mind.

"Don't go fucking up things for Falon and I," He continues, yet I don't turn.

I don't look at him, I won't give him that.

"If I hear you said anything, being homeless would be the least of your problems," His voice breaks on the end betraying his words.

I still stiffen at his harsh warning, his threat but the hurt leaves me.

He is right, I am just a beggar.

We don't get heroes like Zero.

"I understand!" I whisper enough for him to hear and leave his room.

I'm not weak, I'm not strong either, I'm a survivor.

I've lived through hunger for years until my body didn't crave a meal for two days.

I've became resilient to embarrassment when I was left naked for weeks until a lady gave me her clothes from her packet with the tags on, only to see me a few days later and charge me for stealing.

I survived a monster until a family showed me mercy and lifted me up from the pit, I stayed in only to leave me on the side of the road naked, because they were too shit scared to help further.

I survived a pregnancy at sixteen with no money in my pocket while running from a monster that was determined to find me.

I'm still running because I'm a survivor.

So, with one foot in front of the other I walk through the corridor knowing that I will fucking survive the Enforcer of The Satan Sniper's Motorcycle Club.

XIV

1..higher, 72...73..." Ever heard the saying you can take a horse to the water but you can't make it drink?

Spade doesn't believe in that saying.

I know because he told me over and over and over again.

Whenever I'm tired, he pushes.

When I can do no more, he forces.

Spade believes I'm only a human and if he's there he can sure as fuck make me do it.

"81, 82, keep those abs tight we ain't leaving until it's done, 83."

My stomach, neck, back, legs, arms and all the other places I don't know are throbbing, aching as I lift into another curl.

Spade is relentless today. 'It's for your own good' my ass.

My morning started crappy, it's just past 11am and it hasn't gotten better.

"92... I don't see those abs tight Beggar."

The sweat drips from my forehead down into my eye.

My hands are crisscrossed over my chest. Fingers locked firmly over my shoulders as I complete one hundred ab curls.

We're on the top floor aka the training room. Spade is relentless, pushing me for the past two hours. It's closing on midday and normally by this time I'm enjoying the hot tub downstairs while Venus tries to psycho-analyze me.

But Spade kept me here.

"Enough, you're done."

My chest expands and contracts at a rapid speed, my breathing- loud.

Spade turns his back on me, walking across to the treadmill and gets on.

The guy's a machine. He always has excess energy.

It's crazy. Venus should spend more time with Spade than worrying about me.

Clearly I'm not the one with screws loose.

The long tights I'm wearing stick to my ass as I get up. Yesterday Chadley dropped off some new clothes for me. Two jeans, six t-shirts, some panties, two white vests and a pair of training tights. I was so grateful, it was more than any one has ever given me freely.

Killer however seemed disappointed and threw his black card on the bed, which Chadley snatched up in seconds with doughy eyes.

Those said eyes quickly lost some of the sparkle when he told her to give it to Venus.

I had no clue what happened there or why, until Venus popped in after my fiasco with Zero, carrying parcels of more clothes and make up with shoes and so much stuff that I left it all in the room and showed up for training twenty minutes early.

Killer buying me so much stuff, I'm not sure how to deal with it. I don't like to feel that I owe him something and I already know he'll say I owe him nothing.

What he doesn't know is that just hearing those words would break the last bit of humanity in me.

I walk across the blue training mats where the others fight each other at night. I pull the rope as I pass it to go fetch my water on the round plastic table by the door.

The water glides down easily, and I capture the cold feeling that slides down to my belly cooling me down.

A week ago I was living in the frigid cold worrying about my next meal and whether I'll ever escape my monster.

I think back to my morning, was it really that bad?

Today I have a roof over my head, food in my belly and this bottle of water to cool my heated flesh.

Today for the first time in years, my monster's hazel eyes didn't haunt me.

Today for the first time in years I felt awakened. I felt powerful because for the first time in a long time I allowed a man to touch me.

I wanted a man to kiss me, own me. I guess it wasn't crappy after all.

Zero made me feel things in that moment I shouldn't have felt for him.

The Enforcer of The Satan Snipers made me want things I had no business wanting.

He isn't mine.

When I refused to go further, he proved it. His words hurt me because I gave him something, I didn't give anyone else and he rejected it.

But I've heard worse, I've been treated so much worse.

At least he stopped, at least he didn't force me.

I've told myself that over and over again but this tug in my chest just won't ease up.

I'm not a girl that gets to feel like this over a man. I'm used goods, a filthy dirty beggar, a nobody.

I have nothing to offer a man besides my scarred body, dead soul and loads of fucked-upness.

But I felt something today, maybe I'm not as dead as I thought, as dead as my monster honed me to be.

As the thought comes to mind, I chuckle as I finish my water.

How stupid am I? No one can go through what I've been through and still keep their soul.

No one can do what I've done and not lose their goodness.

And besides, Zero made it clear he regrets what we shared. What we felt or I felt was wrong, even though it felt good, explosive.

It was probably nothing for him, he'll get his happy ending with Falon, she's his girl.

Not a filthy beggar like me who's sponging off the club, and getting charity off the people in the house whilst training to be one of them.

Not me, I'm the homeless girl and I mustn't forget that.

If I make a wrong move, I could find myself on the streets again. God knows I don't want that.

I need this.

I need the people more.

It won't be long until my monster finds me. He'll never leave me be.

My mother said that if it felt good doesn't mean it was right.

Zero hates me but I won't hate him, I can't.

He is the reason I'm here, him and Falon.

Which is why I made a new rule from a lesson learnt, Zero is off limits.

The door smacks open and I jump back just in time to miss getting knocked in by the glass door.

"Spade, church now, Prez needs us." Bulls deep frown as he spots me behind the door is something I expect.

The child running from behind him and right into me is something I don't.

I glance down at the boy. He got the bluest eyes I've seen on one other person staring right back at me. His little arms wrap around my waist,

"Uncle Kevin is coming, say I'm not here."

You know that moment where everything happens so fast that you don't get a chance to respond, or say anything? Well that's what is happening now.

"Aron my man." Spade walks up from behind me, and I know why.

He doesn't want me to hurt the kid. I know he'll knock me out before I get a chance but there's no need.

I love kids.

And besides, Bull is standing right here, he could just flick me across the room like a fly and I'll be lights out.

Aron doesn't let go of me though and I smile down at the little boy when he tilts his head to see behind me and his brown hair flops to one side.

"Hey Uncle Thomas, I'm staying with you guys tonight. Aunt D and Ky are coming to pick me up in the morning." Aron's face lights up and I fall hard for the kid when I see the dimple peeping out on his left cheek.

Spade walks up to him and ruffles his hair, careful not to touch me.

Bull clears his throat, "Gotta go man."

Spade's lithe body moves past us. The kid is still holding me around my waist like a life line. I expect him to let me go.

He is holding on to my waist for a few minutes now.

Bull turns to go but stops and stares at Aron, his face softening. Which is a first from the moody biker.

"You stay with this lady, 'til Killer gets you, got it."

Bull doesn't wait for a reply before his heavy footfalls get distant in his retreat.

I peer down at the kid, at a loss. His little fingers tugging my ponytail.

"Your hair is pretty like Aunt Ky. What's your name? Do you like PlayStation? Are you a Dodgers fan? My dad hates the Dodgers! Do you like ice-cream? I only like the caramel fudge, my dad says ice-cream is ice-cream and I shouldn't be fussy just glad that I can have any, but uncle Michael says my dad is a moron because caramel fudge is the best flavor but what would he know 'cause he never tasted it....Bu.."

"Whoa, there kid one question at a time, yeah." His face turns Crimson, and I think the kid is going to start bawling.

Instead he bursts out laughing.

He takes a step back and stares at me. His neck turns to the side like he's observing me and I realize he's just waiting for me to answer.

"Let's see, ah, my name is a secret, but you can call me Beggar."

"Cool name for a cool voice, Beggar," He rolls my name off his tongue like Killer does, I smile at that.

This kid is already topping my favorite people list.

"I don't know what's PlayStation kid and I've never watched sports, but ice-creams good."

"PlayStation is only the coolest thing ever!"

He jumps on the spot.

"Can we go see the horses now, Uncle Kevin is gonna be long, he said you'll take me to see the horses."

I look at the denims he's wearing, they look expensive and the red t-shirt with the crocodile on it I know for a fact is pricey.

Will his uncle be okay with him messing his clothes up?

"How old are you Aron?"

"Six, why?"

"Aron." That voice has us both facing the door.

I'm about to reply when Killer walks in seconds after calling the boy.

I admit a few days ago when I saw him with his piercings and tattoos, he kept hidden the first night, I was speechless and scared spending another night with him, but I know he won't hurt me.

No, he is trying to unravel me.

Killer takes in the scene as only he does, subtle.

Trying to see what he sees I glance to Aron standing a few steps away from me, a big grin plastered on his innocent face.

I'm holding a water bottle in one hand and the other is on my hip.

My vest soaked with sweat.

"Hey, I was packing away your things. Aron's going to be sleeping with us tonight, took a fold up from one of the spare rooms. You cool with that?"

My face spreads into a huge smile at the thought. I have no idea why, maybe it's the fact that I've never gotten to spend time with any kid as an adult.

I feel like I've been offered a moon.

My day started out dreadful but my afternoon is turning out pretty damn good, and the reason why is standing right in front of me and I'm not talking about the little fellow that can't keep his legs still.

I'm talking about the guy that's staring at me with a keen interest that I don't want to guess with what.

"No problem here, I was going to take him to see the horses and for ice-cream." The words leave my mouth at the same time my eyes find Aron's eager ones.

I divert my attention back to Killer waiting for his answer.

He shrugs and gives me another look that I pretend not to notice, but I know I'm in trouble.

Deep trouble.

XV

"Not sure man, spoke to the boys in Mississippi, Loui, Kansas. Dexter even went as far as New York, but we don't wanna be digging in Deno's turf. He'll take it as an insult and we might just find ourselves in a cross fire with the Famiglia," Knight explains.

I trust the guy, he's Italian and a war with Famiglia will put Killer in a tight spot.

We can't have that.

We're all sitting in the basement. Our mind on one purpose, finding Jade. Either she's been kidnapped or worse, dead.

After Beggar fled the room earlier, I destroyed half my bedroom. I was angry at myself for wanting her so bad, for losing control.

I was furious with her for stopping me and also for making me this way.

And those words, what the fuck was I thinking?

I called her the very thing I said wouldn't.

I threatened her.

I was losing my fucking mind, so I did the best thing and jumped on my bike and left.

Went to see my dad. He wasn't there, so I cooled off at the barn.

The need to clear my head and get my shit together was potent.

I'm a grown man acting like a fucking kid who can't keep it in his pants.

Then snapping and blaming a 21-year-old for my attraction to her.

Truth is, I am attracted to Beggar but is it physical or something deeper?

I wish I had a fucking clue. We've barely spoken in these past five days. It's all my fault, I've been a snippy snarling jackass to her since I took her to the park.

I can't even fuck Falon without thinking of Beggar.

I know I should break things off with Falon. I've never cheated on a woman before.

I did it today, I cheated on the woman I wanted to claim. Falon doesn't deserve that, Beggar doesn't deserve it.

What if I didn't leave Falon and Beggar is the one? What if I did leave Falon and Beggar and I didn't work out?

My mind raked up questions and answers, by the time I got back two hours later. It was clear that I had to get to know Beggar.

I had to risk this with Falon and see if there was anything between Beggar and I besides the urge to fuck her.

Five days I've watched Beggar talk and smile with my brothers and the women.

Five days I held off. I continued to ignore her and treat her badly hoping the urge to want her would wane.

But the need, the pull increased.

At the same time, I've been asking myself why her?

Why don't I have these feeling for Falon? I care for Falon enough to marry her, well at least I did a week ago.

Now I'm ready to dump her and I don't feel an ounce of regret.

Fuck my life.

Today Beggar offered to help me even though I deserve the pain from every punch Killer delivered.

I asked him to do it. Storm is supposed to dish out my punishment 'cause he's the VP, but I knew he'll hold back.

Killer wouldn't and he didn't. He knew I needed it.

I hurt her, sent her into a panic because I didn't want to handle the fact that Killer spent his nights in her bed, while I hoped it was me.

I wanted her to turn to me, to smile at me.

Yet, she buckled and fought the second my hands made contact with her body.

I didn't want to believe it, so when she kicked out, I put my hand on her and held her down.

But even though I deserved to suffer she was willing to fix me up, and I didn't hesitate to accept.

While Beggar massaged me, I tried really hard to keep it together.

Her calloused hands on my flesh was too much even for a man like me.

And I caved into the unwanted yet undeniable pull between us, for that moment I consumed her.

The feel of her blunt fingers in my back, her long legs wrapped like a dream around my hips.

Her long hair fanned out on my bed. She was everything and more.

The way she touched me, the way she kissed me. Our mouths fused like two lost souls connecting for the final time.

I've never sucked a woman's tongue so hard or kissed a woman as thorough as I kissed Beggar.

I've never wanted to leave my mark on a woman before, not even Falon.

When she stopped and refused me, I was thinking maybe she was denying me because she was fucking Killer. I didn't give her a chance to prove me right.

I hurt her.

I rejected her. And I didn't think I'll feel like I lost something important.

I didn't think I would feel like I was experiencing grief in the form of a woman I've met five days ago walking out my door without a backward glance.

I need Beggar and I know she needs me too.

I just have to convince her.

I planned to go seek her out when I got back and beg for a chance, but all my plans fled to shit when I got the call from Houston and that was that.

I hadn't had a chance to think about anything besides finding out who took one of our own.

"Who was the first person to know she was missing?" Killer asks Storm from his corner in the room.

"Mercy, Jade promised to call her yesterday when she got to Texas City. They were supposed to meet there before joining up with Moscow and Trader somewhere in Sugar land," Spade adds from behind me.

The brother is good friends with Jade. He never claimed her but I know they've been sleeping in the same bed for a couple months now.

This shit must be hard for him.

I listen attentively to all that they say whilst my fingers work furiously on my laptop.

"Her last known location was Texas City, just picked her up on a traffic cam, shot was taken23 hours ago," I say to them before I meet Storm's alert gaze.

Rounder was having a bad day today with the chemo so Falon and Chadley took him for a check-up.

Texas followed behind them.

My VP is in charge of this one. So, he is going to have to make the call.

"Prepare to ride tomorrow. I'm not saying Houston can't find our girl, but you are the best hunter we got man," Storm says to me.

Which is the truth.

It's how I got my name.

Zero failed missions, zero missed kills, zero unfound missing persons. And for the last 8 years since I got the name it has remained, zero.

"I'll go with him," Spade demands.

No one argues to that.

"Get Falon to go to Barfa this weekend and speak to Kandra, maybe she heard something. Knight and Killer, you stay, got a bad feeling about this. Don't want the girls and Prez without protection. Snake and I are going on a little racing trip tomorrow night. What do you say man?" I feel Snakes energy across the fucking room.

The guy loves speed of any kind.

"Bull needs to shadow the girls. Venus don't tell them shit. Falon is the only one who needs in. At least until we know more got it."

"Yeah." Venus has been taking it bad since we found out, she was the one to send Jade on the mission.

Jade was up for getting her tat.

We voted her in a few months back but Rounder said to hold off until she sorted stuff out with her sister, Abby.

"This was supposed to be a walk in the park, a simple meet up with Mercy, collect some evidence for a client then come back to Kanla. I think the question is not whether she was taken but where was she taken," Snake points out.

"And who the fuck took her!" Spade growls from behind me.

"There's not many people who'll touch a Satan Sniper. I don't think we should rule out the entire Cosa Nostra. The Famiglia yeah, they're too powerful to even bother with that shit, but the outfit is still into trafficking. Jade has a history in that world, it's clear someone could've seen her, recognized her. She did after all kill a dozen of their men."

Killer voices exactly what I've considered except,

"We are forgetting one other person who could want her dead."

They all stare at me.

"Mayor Grison."

Storm considers the implications this would cause but his eyes harden.

"Killer, you up brother." Killer nods but his face looks grim and I know why.

His brother's son is spending the night at the Clubhouse. He hardly gets to see the kid since he moved in with his dad in New York.

Killer sees my intent to go in his place but shakes his head at me.

"Let's get Jade home." Storm bangs the hammer on the table.

The mumble agreements from all of us as we walk up the cemented steps to the main floor dies down when Spade opens the door.

Music is blasting through the Clubhouse and there's not a soul in sight.

Crazy girl by Eli young band is playing, but it's not playing from the speakers but sang by a feisty 19-year-old trouble maker.

Storm's feet carry him faster than all of us to where the music is coming from, well more to who the music is coming from.

Knight groans and Bull follows the man to the bar.

Venus smiles next to me but doesn't move, neither does Killer whose lips are pressed in a harsh line.

"Your sisters here, what's up your ass?" I ask him.

Killer snickers,

"My sister is here dumbass." He follows the direction Storm went in.

"His pride is a bit bruised. Beggar rejected his gifts this morning and hid out with Spade for over two hours in the training room."

Venus shakes her head.

"Who does that? She's something."

"Didn't know they were hooking up," I reply, feigning disinterest but inside I'm fucking boiling with rage.

And this is the last thing I need now if my head is going to be clear to find Jade.

"Not yet." She sounds too certain.

"How do you know?"

The music stops along with the singing as I ask that question. At the same time Venus's violet knowing gaze settles on me.

A small smirk stretches across her face.

"Same way I know you're jealous, observation."

I glare at her and grind my teeth knowing I'm in a rut.

Denying Venus's suspicions or 'observation' is like telling Killer's sister, Kylie to shut up, pointless.

"And what is it you have observed regarding Killer, Doc." I keep the sarcasm to a minimum but I can't deny it isn't there.

But Venus as usual doesn't give a shit.

"He spent 18 minutes extra in the shower yesterday plus another 18 this morning. Killer doesn't take thirty minutes in the shower washing his crack dumbass."

She saunters off, her hair open and swishing as she walks away.

And that's one of the many reasons I wish Venus was a guy so I could knock her out without having the fear of getting castrated.

Deciding to ignore the loud squeals coming from the lounge area, I head for the kitchen for an early lunch. The faint smell of roasted chicken that Chadley made this morning wafts through the air and my stomach growls.

They should be back by now.

I open the double door to the kitchen and Chadley is bent over the bucket, squeezing the mop.

Her hair hidden underneath that grey woolen hat her ma gave her last Christmas. I thought she threw it out.

She's the only girl in the club I haven't ever fucked because she's Falon's cousin, so off limits in my book.

That doesn't mean we ain't friends.

I walk past her and smack her hard on the ass. I'm caught off guard as she assaults me with the mop.

First a hard swat to the leg.

"Stop, shit." My voice booms through the kitchen.

But she doesn't listen, and I have my arm across my face blocking the crazy woman.

When she lifts the broom to hit me again, I grab the mop. "Enough of this shit," I bellow.

"You had no business slapping my ass." The unmistakable voice sends a sick thrill through me.

But the death glare and the fact that she's probably plotting my murder reminds me to tread with caution.

"Didn't know it's you Beauty, thought you were Chadley."

She gives me a doubtful look that I return with a straight one.

Yeah baby, bring it on. We stay like this, in a staring competition until Killer walks in.

"What's going on?" He's asking me but his eyes are trained on Beggar who has since dropped her black depths to the white kitchen floor.

Like a true submissive.

The thought fills my mind for the umpteenth time. Am I wasting my time? I watch Killer.

His need to own her is as clear as my need to protect her, save her.

He won't wait much longer before he owns her. Question is, does Beggar want to be his property?

"Nothing, no biggie," She mumbles and starts walking away toward the outside door.

I'm not sure how or when but I'm starting to understand why I go after her.

"You just wait a minute."

Her answer is to walk faster away toward the lake.

"Beauty."

Her body spins around. "Don't call me that, it's Beggar, just Beggar, you had no problem calling me that earlier."

She doesn't raise her voice but I can tell she really wants to.

What's holding her back, what will it be like to see the fire light her black pools up? Does her skin flush when she's angry?

I can't deny this pull toward her, I won't, not anymore.

"I'm sorry."

The loose denim jeans she's wearing hangs low on her hip bone and hides the slope of her body. The curve of her ass though gets the best spotlight.

Her hollowed narrow face loses the fight I saw spark in her.

"Why are you following me Zero. Haven't you said enough?!" The question is a rhetorical one.

I take a step closer to her, and watch as she instinctively wraps her arms around her chest.

"You keep walking away from me, what the fuck am I supposed to do?"

"Easy, don't follow me. The point of me walking away is to get away, from you."

"You know for a girl who barely spoke a word to me this week and keeps walking away you awfully chatty."

"Well maybe I just have something to say."

Her snarky manner makes me grin as I close the distance between us.

"Yeah, well so do I. For starters to answer that earlier question, I can't help following you."

Her eyes search my own, her guard impenetrable.

The truth in my eyes is right there for her to see and when she does, I watch in complete fascination as she lowers those high walls.

Beggar doesn't move as I take another step closer. Close enough to touch her.

She lifts her black gaze to me and I get that same fucking knot in the pit of my stomach as the hairs at the back of my nape rise.

"I'm an asshole Beauty. A jealous asshole."

She frowns at me, her straight nose scrunching up in confusion.

The downward curve of her lips straightens, it's so subtle that you'll never notice unless you really know her.

The sun from the left, heating the side of her face with a yellow glow.

"You, Jealous?" She snorts.

"What's wrong with that?" I touch her jaw, a light whisper of my fingers and she gasps taking a step back the second I make contact.

I can't help the glint in my gaze, watching her.

I watch her readying to flight as she checks the time on a black watch on her wrist, but not really checking it, just making a show of doing it.

At any other moment it'll be the funniest thing watching her squirm but not now.

I don't want her to walk away from me.

"I gotta get back to Aron." She goes to turn her back on me.

I grip her elbow and pull her back to my front stopping her retreat.

Her ass is right there on my cock that's hardening fast.

She's my perfect fit. Her head touches my chin as she fits to my body like she was meant to be there.

Like I've held her before a thousand times over.

I close my eyes at the overload of emotions rushing in me.

And for the first time my arms lock around Beggar.

She shakes and fights me, her sneakers kicking me on my legs as her blunt nails scratch my arms violent enough that it's already reddening.

I bend my head and whisper the command in her ear, "No!"

"Please just let me go, let me go, let me go..." She says it over and over again, and I just hold her tighter knowing the answer to that question.

"I can't Beauty, that's the problem. I can't let you go."

The rise and fall of her chest increase, but I won't let her go. I need her to calm to me.

I have to trust my gut that I'm doing the right thing, it's never let me down before.

And I won't doubt myself now when I'm facing off the hardest battle of my life.

Not when I'm going for Beggar's trust.

"Shsh... I got you Beauty, you safe with me, you know I'll never hurt you, sssshhh, you safe, it's me Zero. You wanna know my real name, it's Logan. My dad said it was meant for girls but my ma insisted she name me." I rock her slowly in my arms as she mumbles words and nods her head at my small talk but I don't let her go. *I can't.*

My arms serve as a cage but also a shield around her.

The airy scent I've come to know is Beggars, wafts through my nose as I sway her in my arms.

Her shakes become weaker until she's just still, but I don't give her the choice to go under,

"Wanna know why I call you Beauty?"

"No," she croaks softly.

"When I first saw you, it was your eyes that held me captive. I've never seen black eyes on such pale skin before. I just stood there staring at you from all the way across the road, do you know that?"

She shakes her head, and I kiss her hair inhaling her.

"When I look at you it reminds me of a story my ma told me, about a horse named black beauty, a wild horse that wouldn't be tamed but no one cared because it was just so beautiful to look at, like you."

She starts fighting me when I say it.

Her head thrashes from side to side getting me in the mouth.

I taste the copper on my tongue but it's nothing to her words, they slay me.

"I'm not beautiful, I'm a filthy dirty beggar, I'm a filthy dirty beggar, let me go please, I'm a filthy, dirty, beggar."

"No!" My voice is firm and stern as I rest my head on her shoulder.

"You know I can't do that; I'm never going to be able to let you go. You got me in fuckin' spades woman. I know I hurt you this morning, you gave me something special and I fucked up.

But I came back, had to clear my head, think shit through, and you know what I thought,

you know who I thought about? You.

Who's the one I want? You.

Who is the one I care about? You again.

Who would I die for? You.

I'm going to leave Falon because there's no point wasting her time. And you and I are going to explore this between us, 'cause Beauty this what we have, this thing it's fuckin' crazy. Somethin' we gotta hold onto, this don't happen for anyone, but it's happening between us and I know you got some hang ups and I got them too, but we gonna work on that together okay. You gotta trust me, you gotta trust this."

I'm silent as I glance up into the setting sun, and the woman made just for me wrapped in my arms,

"You gotta give me a chance to catch you when you heading for that cliff, yeah. Because baby I'm gonna catch you, there's no fuckin' way around it."

She whimpers and I know she's listening. I know what I'm saying, I know what I'm feeling,

I know she's feeling it too. I wanna spend my night in this woman's arms. I'm done wasting time.

Falon and I will never have this, whatever the fuck it is, because I can only have it with this woman. This is the woman that's made for me.

"You gonna give us a chance, yeah, and you gonna let me show that whoever hurt you, whoever did this to you they will NEVER touch you again. I'll never let them hurt you again Beauty, as bright as the sun shines, I'll hunt the motherfucker down and I'll kill him."

She whimpers and I know she's gonna clock out, but it's fine, because she's mine now and when she falls, I catch her in my arms just like I said I would.

I make my way back into the Clubhouse but stop when I see Killer.

He doesn't say anything, I don't say fuck all too. But our eyes say it for us.

He's going to back off, he knows what I have with Beggar is something. But I also know that if I fuck it up, I won't get a chance with her again.

He'll own her whether she wanted it or not. And I won't be able to stop him. No one will.

XVI

The Clubhouse is not a place I want to be picking David's son up from, but it's the only time little Aron gets to see Kevin, my older brother aka Killer, argh.

I'm not judging, I'm seriously not, okay, maybe just a little. There's a lot of names in the dictionary to use that mean killer, why use the actual thing. Come on.

I shake my head at my way ward thoughts, and check my recently green sparkled nail polish, Ivy crush. It's wicked.

The kitchen door opens with a bang and a scarred grim reaper walks out with a limp female in his arms, bride style.

Her hair is like a black curtain of strands, a lot like mine except, well it's not. That's dead hair.

Something I'm so fixing.

"What shiny new toy does the big bad beast have there?" I drawl my words lazily.

I used to do it to piss my momma off. Over the years she made it her personal mission in 'assisting' me to ditch the glitch or famously known as the 'Kylie twang.'

She was of course successful but every now and then it comes out to play.

What can I say? I'm a Bray.

My eyes scan over the biker's black leather pants, it's old and terrible, but his black t-shirt is perfect. I bought that for him.

I'm about to say as much when I'm startled at the soft gaze, he gives the sleeping form that is undoubtedly unconscious by the angle of her neck.

I've known the Enforcer of The Satan Snipers for five years and he's never looked at a woman like that, not even when he was with tiny Falon. Never liked that tiny bitch.

"She's our new prospect. A hello to you too Kylie. I'm great and how are you doing as well Kylie." He lifts his head to me.

The scar under his eye makes the one eye seem smaller compared to the other.

It used to have me cringing and flinching at the biker, but over the years he has become one of the very few friends I have.

"You know how I feel about pleasantries Zero. I'll follow you up."

He shakes his head with a smile and moves toward the stairs, already knowing I'm a lost cause.

I hate greeting people, I hate meeting people, I hate saying goodbye to people.

Yes, there's a lot of things I hate, I can afford to.

If you don't like me, well scratch that of course you going to like me, I'm Kylie Bray.

My momma said hate is a strong word to use. So, I asked her why if it's how I feel.

She said true hate is something that has to run deep, it has to be unforgiving.

I told her it was exactly how I felt about her leaving me for three years, without a note, message and goodbye. She didn't even say hello when she returned. Well that just had her leaving the room, end of conversation.

I trail behind the big biker, my boots heavy on the dark grey carpeted stair case.

"You saw my Kevin?"

"He's gone out, why what's up? You need something?"

I fling my hair to the side as my denim covered legs climb higher up. I almost groan as the masculine products fill my nose as we pass the bathroom.

Finally, I'm away from the disinfectant clogging my brains downstairs.

We stop at the eighth door.

I open the white princess cut door for him to go in first with his damsel.

"Nope, came to see if Aron wanted to join Diamond and me for the horse trails and check on Storm but they both gone riding, wanted to see Kevin before I head out but he ain't here."

"Ain't gonna see him now Ky."

I sigh at what a waste of my time and tilt my head to the side as a thought saddles up in my mind.

Watching him lay her down on the bed reminds me of the conversation I had with Kevin yesterday.

"The reason why my brother doesn't want me over. She's Beggar, right?" I drawl in a thick Texan accent.

I stare at the beautiful girl. The one my heartless brother spoke about to David.

I was in David's office when he got the call. He had the phone on speaker while he worked.

When Kevin said he met a girl and she was homeless who insisted on the name Beggar, curiosity plagued me and I jumped in my ride with a nagging Diamond and drove six hours from Liston Hills to Kanla a day before schedule. It was a well worth trip. My brother has never mentioned a woman in his life.

And I can see why this one is different. Nice pale skin, dark hair that is as long as mine and pitch black just like mine but whereas hers is months away from dying, mine is full straight and shiny. It's also the color of Natasha's hair, Natasha's skin. My father's 16-year-old daughter, my halfsister.

Kevin ain't foolin' nobody but himself.

"Yup, she's knocked out, probably going to be for a couple hours. But I don't wanna leave her alone. Up for some t.v.?"

"No thanks, gotta get back to Diamond. She needs to eat, can't leave her too long," I shrug.

He doesn't need me to elaborate, he knows that Diamond will go days without eating or bathing while she gets stuck in the web of her mind unless someone forces her to do it.

Unlike my brother Michael who has control of his 'genius' and uses it rather than let's his mind use and control him.

Diamond is the ugly and dark side of a living genius.

She's the one the t.v. shows won't tell you about.

She's the genius that the governments capture and keep in deserted places to carry out their sick work.

Diamond is a weapon.

She is what you won't see coming. She acts normal for all intents but I know she is anything but.

When the urge comes it could be months of her stuck in the labyrinth that's her mind.

But it's better than her getting angry.

A cold shiver licks my spine at the thought. My feet take me to the white blinds, passing the bed and I open it as my mind clouds on memories of Diamond.

How do I keep her safe, how am I going to keep her sane?

Diamond is slipping away; I feel it every time she gets that call and I don't know how to stop them. They using her and they will continue to do so until she's nothing.

The motorbikes lined in a neat row take up my attention as my mind runs track.

I'm not sure how long I'm standing here when a noise in the room captures my attention.

It starts as a deep gurgle like choking.

You know the sound a person makes when they can't breathe, yeah, this one is worse.

My head naturally spins to the direction of the noise, the bed.

The vision in front of me has me at a standstill. I've always believed myself strong and resilient, a fixer.

But this, this is something I can't fix, this is something that I can't be strong and watch.

This is a breaking point to witness.

This is torture.

What I see before me will become the reason I make a choice in the next few months that will take me on my path of ruin. A path so dark I will never see the end.

I will become the monster your parents warned you about, because it was at this moment that I opened my eyes.

This moment my world became unlocked to that which I was too naïve to believe.

It was at this place, a Clubhouse in Kanla on a sunny Friday that I placed my first foot in the fire.

This is when I began my journey. This is when I became Frost.

Beggar lays writhing, her back bending in to a deep arch as her legs splay open.

Her hands wrap around her long neck choking herself, until her face is blue, as she screams, and screams her tortured soul out with one word, Padrone, *owner*.

Zero is not here, he left sometime while I was in my mind.

Her top rides up as she writhes but still choking herself.

And I stand here, still, frozen, until I see the redness on her torso. A step or two I take until I'm right there. My knees touching the shaking bed.

I snap out of whatever it is, and the first thing I see clearly is that her skin is changing color, she's going to choke herself into unconsciousness.

I spin into action jumping on the bed and go to grab her arms pulling them off her neck.

Her high pitch scream rings in my ears as she fights me.

Pulling it back, as I pull her hands to me, her body is like a wild beast.

"Zero," I scream, "Zero."

The door bolts open seconds later, but it's those seconds I take my eyes off her, and those seconds that spin my world on its axis.

Beggar opens her mouth like something is getting shoved inside and it doesn't take a college graduate to guess what she's picturing, what she must be reliving.

Zero pulls her hands easily into one of his. Her wild movement lifts her top up and the branded burn I see almost makes my knees buckle.

I can't believe what I'm seeing but after I see it again my eyes widen, there's no doubt what it is.

Zero lifts her up and crushes her to his chest.

"Sssshhh, Beauty, I got you, it's me Zero, you need to wake up now, okay, wake up Beauty. Sssshhh."

He is so strong, his words soothing, his voice firm, but I see the horror on his paled skin. I see it as I feel mine.

I rush out of the room and barely make it to the bathroom before I spill my guts out in the toilet.

My mind boggles. He said they didn't do it; he said his people never took women. They would never traffic, never enslave. He lied, I know this, I know this as I know that the mark burnt into that girl's stomach is the mark of his kind, the mark of possession, the mark of a slave.

The mark of the *Famiglia*.

I don't waste time looking at the couple. I don't waste time doing anything.

I don't even rinse out my bile tasting mouth. I take the steps three at a time and rush to my gold Mercedes. My keys in my hand clicking buttons before I slide in, turn the ignition and get the hell out of there.

My foot hits the gas and I speed to the hotel. I get my phone from the compartment in the center of the car and dial my baby brother.

It rings three times.

"Don't tell me you miss my ass," His way of greeting.

"You alone?" I ask through the car speakers.

He's quiet for a minute,

"Yeah, hit me."

My eyes on the road, I push the cruise control, and sit back.

"I heard Kevin talking about a girl yesterday, came to Kanla with Diamond a day early to see her for myself. Her name is Beggar by the way."

"Yeah, heard D asking Michael to do some digging. Some homeless girl they picked up in Washington."

"Yup, but when I get there, she's unconscious in Zero's arms. A few minutes after he put her on the bed, she starts having some sort of seizure or nightmare. I'm not sure what the hell was that. I've never seen that fucked up shit Jace."

My hand hits the hooter in frustration, this is my brother I don't hide from my family.

"Fuck, I can't even talk to Diamond about this because she's having her benders again."

He's silent and I sigh, shit, me and my big mouth.

"Sorry, I wanted to tell you but I don't want you worrying when you got enough shit going on."

"Hey, it's okay, I get it." Jace says.

"You need to drop that smack down Jace, it's not your fault, if you didn't tell them they would've figured it out."

His silence just pisses me off. I make another turn and head down toward the supermarket.

"You were kidnapped, it's not your fault okay, Diamond is doing this for you don't be ungrateful and squander your life away. You dropping out of a private school to go to public is one thing. Riding yourself with guilt is something completely different."

I take a right at the four way and carry on straight.

"Can we just drop it. What do you need from me?"

I sigh again,

"Beggar has a mark on her stomach and brand, guess from who."

"Biker or Outlaw."

"Worse, it's from good ole Vincent's clan."

"What. The. Fuck."

"My thoughts exactly, it's their mark, the one they brand on the soldiers and their possessions."

I don't tell him that where they put the mark makes a difference.

"Whatcha need Ky?"

"I need to find out who the fuck is Beggar but without drawing attention, so no P.I's. Can you pull it off?"

"Yeah."

"Okay, how?"

"One word, golf."

"Golf?" I park the car in front of the only hotel in this small dead town.

"Yup, Sabastian has recently become a fully pledged member, got his inheritance and full rights to the company."

"Okaaay," I drag out the word.

"Remember the Kents."

I groan, "How can I forget!"

He chuckles through the speaker, so not funny.

"Yeah well, Dexter's dad died last year, so he's taken over all of Kent's holdings including..."

"Being Delroy's bitch," I finish for him with a smirk on my face.

"Yup, if anyone can get it done, it'll be him. I'll talk to Sabs and get back to you by tomorrow."

"I knew I loved you for a reason." I end the call and hop out of the car.

I get into the 4-star dump of a hotel to go feed my friend while she creates another mass destruction weapon for the U.S government while losing apart of herself in the process with one thought in my mind.

How the fuck am I going to get close to Vincent Stone?

XVII

My head rests under a soft pillow, but my body is engulfed in strong warm arms.

I'm safe.

I must be under angel wings because I've never felt safe before.

Did I do it? I ask myself.

Am I dead?

Did I finally take the short cut?

No, I scream, *no*, I can't be, I'm not done. I'm not ready to die yet.

"Sssshhh, Beauty, I got you. You safe," I hear the voice.

It's familiar, welcoming, but frightening at the same time. I wanna run from this person, but don't wanna leave.

Why?

Will I hurt him too? No, I don't hurt anyone. I scream, "I'm a filthy, dirty beggar. Filthy dirty beggar."

"Wake up Beauty, you need to WAKE UP," The command has my eyes fluttering.

I take a deep breath in as my body sighs with unaltered relief. I'm not dead. I'm still surviving.

The green eyes I stare into brings it all back.

Why I'm *here*.

His words. "*I'm never going to be able to let you go.*"

Zero surrounding me. "*Wanna know why I call you Beauty?*"

Zero's arms locking me to his chest. "*You gotta give me a chance to catch you when you heading for that cliff.*"

My knees buckling when he calls me Beauty.

My undoing. "*I'll hunt the motherfucker down and I'll kill him.*"

I'm flat on my back, Zero is looming partially above me. His arms are locking around my waist and back, forming a caged circle around my mid-section.

His weight on his elbow under my back is holding him up as he looks directly into my eyes.

Why the fuck am I letting him hold me?

It's like he can see it, my indecision. He can see my battle and releases me.

Pulling his hand out from under me.

I crawl backward until my spine is flat to the head board, knees to my chest, hands on my toes, head to my knees but it doesn't touch, it mustn't.

My hair falls to the front hiding my face, apart from one eye.

My comfort, my blanket.

I don't like how he sees me, how he looks at me. At least now I'm protected from his perceptive stare.

"You shouldn't be in here. Where's Killer?" My throat pains, so my question comes out deeper and drier.

He sighs, I hear it but I don't see it. I'm chicken.

I ain't gonna look at him.

"Killer isn't going to be staying in here with you anymore Beauty."

My head snaps up when I feel him move and stop in front of me.

One of his leather covered thighs hang off the bed while the other foot folds in, so his sock covered foot is touching the inside of his thigh, a few spaces away from me.

I'm not surprised by Killer wanting to distance himself.

I'm too fucked up.

The guy probably got sick of my nightmares. I know they're bad, I've seen the evidence, lived through it.

Killer isn't one to care for much. I'm surprised it lasted so long.

I'm not sure why it gets to me.

I expected it.

Nothing good works out for me.

I ain't lucky.

Why did I think different?

Why did I think Killer understood? Maybe he did understand, maybe he just didn't want anything more to do with my shit.

"Okay, no Killer, now get out." I say it calmly but inside I'm a wreck.

Killer helps but so did something else before I met The Satan Snipers. It was my fault that I got too close. *Stupid girl.*

"Excuse me?" What he's really saying is, What the fuck.

I should laugh at how shocked he is, but I don't find anything funny.

Zero is not a handsome man, at all. He is sexy with dangerous eyes, succubus lips and a chiseled face that cuts you up piece by piece until you are shattered.

I don't need to be cut up and I most definitely don't need to be shattered.

It's clear Zero wants to fix me. If I allow him to waste his time, he will leave Falon for me, a filthy, dirty beggar because he is foolish.

I broke years ago, my pieces so small that I became unfixable.

What Zero feels is getting his dick wet, and being my hero, and what I feel is fear, horrific deadly fear.

"Get. Out. Now. I want you away from me. I don't want you, all that you said I don't want it. I don't even like you, so GET. OUT."

I'm grateful for the venom in my voice, it hides the tremor that rips another piece of my dead soul but this is for the best.

I am not the girl for this Enforcer, sweet Falon is. I won't come between two people.

There is no future with me and this Enforcer. Why can't he see that? I'm a beggar for fuck sake.

Didn't he hear when I told him that? Didn't he get the memo when I shot those guys?

There is no redemption for my sins, my soul died a long time ago.

My humanity is next.

I don't drop my gaze, and he doesn't drop his shocked one either. And then we are at a stare off and I'm sure I'm going to win this; I just know it.

Zero's eyes become smaller the longer I hold.

The one with the scar ticks as he lifts his finger to rub the scar. My stomach tightens at the hard glint he bestows upon me.

"No," He growls tersely, "I'm not fuckin' going anywhere. You and I are happenin.'"

My gaze narrows and I do the stupidest thing. I piss the beast off.

My legs kick out and my feet hit him in the chest. He makes a "oomph" sound, grabs my ankles and splits my legs open.

He got one ankle locked in each of his big hands.

"Let me go you asshole." I try to twist but his grip is strong.

"I don't want you!" I scream from my tortured throat.

I snicker when he tightens his hold of my ankles in warning.

"Too fuckin' bad, woman."

"I don't give second chances." I glare at him as my hair falls out of my face.

He laughs, and it's evil and arrogant.

"Tough shit woman, 'cause you'll be giving me lots of chances. You know what else you'll be giving me?" He pulls my ankles toward him and in a swift move his fingers are curling around my thighs and I'm being lifted up until I'm straddling him.

My air leaves me and my mouth gaps open at how quick he just manhandled me.

His hungry gaze drinks me up and a hot need rises in my body as I close the gap between our lips.

Zero moves fast, and I find my ass cheeks under his hands before my lips make contact with his.

My fingers find his neck, curling around the back in a tight grip.

I dart my tongue with a tentative glide, just for a taste, but Zero has other plans and crashes his mouth to mine, lips to lips.

His tongue pushes into my mouth, and tangles with mine for dominance. Zero is a man certain of his actions.

His kiss is experienced and pure poison.

I kiss this man and he kisses me back.

Our lips mash together, firm and sure as our tongues tangle and suck on each other's tongue in an erotic dance of wills.

Zero doesn't squeeze my ass as he did earlier, he doesn't grind into me with the hot rod coming from his leather pants right there by my denim covered opening.

He just devours my mouth like he owns me, like he knows me.

And I find myself kissing him like I adore him, like he could be mine, like I could have the possibility.

I feel so much in this kiss.

His hands on my ass, my head tilted to one side, and his to the other.

I feel all that he wants to tell me, all that he wants to say.

It's a good five or so minutes later that he breaks the kiss with small pecks on the corner of my mouth and I find myself smiling at him as I open my eyes.

"You an idiot if you think a kiss will change my mind. You want to save me, but I can't be saved Zero, I don't want redemption. I got nothing to give you but pain, don't you see it. Falon is a good girl, she's the girl for you, not some fil.."

"Don't you dare fuckin' say it woman," He snaps, at the same time his hands squeeze my ass in warning.

"And stop telling me what's right for me. I can figure that shit out on my own. You gonna give me everything, Beauty, just like I'm going to take it and want more and besides that wasn't a kiss, that was a taste of things to come. This ass is mine now, don't you know?"

The char grin marking his wet lips is over boiling with manly pride and I find myself being willed to agree, just for this moment.

This moment where I'm just a girl and he is just a man.

"Don't be scared of me, you know I won't hurt you."

He rubs his hands up and down my ass cheeks as we stare at each other.

I realize the position I'm in. My knees are holding me up as I straddle him and I got my hands around his neck massaging the knots out and I'm not freaking out.

There's no monster here.

"Thanks for that." I say, but he doesn't know how much I mean it.

He has quietened my monster even if it's just for a while. It's not the first time too and I'm truly grateful.

Even if I know that we can't be, for the simple fact that I am not just a woman looking at this biker.

I can never be his when I'm still fighting the chains holding me prisoner. The chains put there by another man who made me love him, made me need him until I had nothing left but a shred of humanity, just enough to keep living, keep surviving.

I watch Zero's eyes glaze with ownership, like I'm his possession and I feel a stir of something planted deep within me.

Staring into his depths I know that I want to be his, I want to be owned by a hero just one time, but just like that I'm reminded that I am someone else's possession, a beautiful monster, who will never let me go.

He will always search for me; he will always find me.

"Tu *sei mia mendicante.*" *You are mine beggar.*

Those were the last words he whispered to me, two years ago, the last time he found me.

The thought should scare me, should leave me in fear but I find myself resigned.

I had 5 years to accept my fate. 5 years to accept my chains.

I hide my turmoil as I stare into this man's harsh face, this man that keeps the monster away.

By doing that I also hide my fate but I'm determined to live in this moment, for once I just want to live in this moment. *Can't I just have that?*

"You gonna jump on the back of my bike, gotta meet my dad woman."

I'm taken back by that and the serious look in his eyes.

I drop my hands from his neck and cross them over my chest.

"That doesn't sound like a question Logan."

He smiles at the mention of his name and I fight my own.

"Wasn't asking you a question woman, just thinking out loud."

I shrug, holding in my laugh, "You gonna call me Beggar?"

He's silent for a moment and I pay attention to the curve of his strong jaw and not his eyes.

So, I'm startled when he throws his head back and laughs.

"Nice try." He smacks my ass, and the sound resonates through me as my body comes aflame.

He sees it, he feels it and does it again on the same ass cheek.

My pussy clenches and I grip his rough face in my palms, my mouth going to his.

The knock on the door stops me. I go to wiggle off him, but the bastard smacks me again.

"Don't you dare move, we not done."

"You want them to check you with the low life," I tug on his earlobe.

He arches his brow, "If you talking 'bout the one with her ass in my hands, hell yeah. Come in Knight."

The door opens, and I don't move as Spade and Knight come walking in like they own the place. They're both take in our position which is obvious and maybe if I weren't me, I'd be embarrassed or some shit, but again I'm not. So, I stare at the men, first at Knight's confused frown, who is the Sergeant-at-arms for The Satan Snipers, then at Spade's haunted powder blues that are on me.

It's clear that something is going on with the club.

I picked up on it this morning. This is just confirming my suspicion.

"Falon is looking for you man she's at the stables, says she needs a ride to Barfa, and Beggar your shifts on in twenty. Also got brothers coming in from Houston, Mercy is coming with a few others from Sugar land, gotta set beds up," Spade says, before he storms out.

I'm confused at Spade's need to flee. I stare at Zero, his eyes watch the man, remorseful at his brother's retreating form.

Knight however sits on the bed behind me.

"This really breaks my heart Beggar, I really thought I was getting in there any day now."

I turn my head to the Italian biker. Knight is a charming male, a true Italian, a lady's man.

My hands leave Zero's neck, his stay firmly on my ass, a sign of possession. If only.

I see the playful glint on the Sergeant-at-arms and maybe it's because I'm in a compromised position, or maybe it's because I just kissed Zero, and he practically claimed me in front of his brothers but I reciprocate.

My voice drops with my eyes as I stare intently at Knight, trapping him in my black soul, "And where exactly is there, Cavaliere."

The word rolls off my tongue easily. Knight is shocked and quietens as I watch him, waiting.

"Sei Italiano."

I drop my gaze at his statement, there's no way I can answer that. I should've kept my mouth shut, stupid me.

I didn't think one word is a big deal.

Zero clears his throat and I face him.

"Are you? Italian."

"No, I just know a few words is all."

Zero let's go of me, and I scoot over mindful Knight is behind me, careful not to touch him.

"Why are you lying?" Zero accuses in a soft voice as his feet go to the carpeted floor.

"How do you know I'm lying, where's the proof?" I say but avoid his gaze.

I could lie to his face, it's easy, but I don't want to answer this question. I don't want to lie either but I'm backed in a corner.

My guard rises and my defenses grow with every second.

I can't reveal things about myself without revealing the very things that could get me found.

"Le Donne italiane non imploro." *Italian woman don't beg.*

I pretend I don't understand, I pretend I'm clueless of what Knight is promising in his words. And it's not that he will look after me.

"Keep Fal busy for me. I'll be down in a minute." With those parting words from the Enforcer, Knight leaves and Zero and I are alone.

"Look at me Beauty." I want to disobey him, I want to push him away but I can't, and I find myself lifting my chin up to face the Enforcer's blank, unreadable features.

"I don't mind you keeping stuff to yourself, but there's some stuff you gotta tell me. I'm not saying tell everyone. I'm saying you gotta tell me. No matter what we feel, how strong it is, we won't work if you keep lying, that shit doesn't work with me Beauty, I can't trust easily, I won't." He doesn't realize that he is touching the scar under his eye when he says those words, but I see it.

Something dark steals his sweetness, steals the man that held me hostage outside. Something dark takes away the man that just kissed me like I was his. And for a moment I am taken back to a memory of someone, but I can't get a face.

My survivor instincts kick in at the hard set of his jaw and the unreadable penetrating gaze of his eyes.

I should question his sudden change of mind, or his ultimatum but I don't. I'm used to this, the worst kind of bad luck. I have experienced it many times before. My monster stole my soul and replaced it with chains, but he also made me stronger.

He shredded my pride and taught me to expect the worse.

"Don't believe in hope Beggar, you'll always be disappointed."
His words ring true again.

I wanted a few moments to pretend and I got it.

Now I have to let it go.

So, it isn't hard when I smile at the biker.

Staring him dead in the eyes, I tell him,

"We all lie, but It's the reason we do it which counts. I'll give you one truth, just one, but you can't ask me my name."

"Will I ever be able to trust you?" His question rolls off his tongue and out of his mouth without thinking.

I get up from the bed, my hair falling around my shoulders, down to my waist.

"That's a question only you and time will know the answer to Zero."

I move toward the door and pause.

My back to the Enforcer.

"Thank you for that kiss but I cannot be your woman Zero, because the same monster I run from is the only one who'll ever own me."

"I'll kill him." He replies with so much hatred and promise that another woman would've believed him but hope is a fool's courage.

I spin around, my smile weak.

"My fate was sealed years ago Zero, killing him won't save me."

I walk out the door of my room and down the steps knowing that I did the right thing.

It's for his own safety, for my last shred of humanity. I can't be saved and I can't let myself get hurt either, I won't.

Zero's moods and issues run deep. I didn't get on Storm's bike to find a man.

I got on his bike to run from one. *Stupid girl.*

I make my way to the bar, passing the noisy bikers in the t.v. room,

"Yo Beggar, get me a beer will you sweet thang," Texas says as I pass him.

"You want one too Bull?" I ask the big biker sitting quietly on the corner sofa nursing a glass of Amber liquid.

He's the shortest one from all the men but has the biggest muscles. His hair is tied back today making his half Mexican blood stand out.

When he leaves his hair open which is most of the time, the guy is opposing. He is the one I've spoken too least and when we do it's clipped and terse.

He hates me for some reason but I still find myself checking up on him. It's a no brainer that he has dark demons lurking in his head, like me.

He grunts his reply as I turn the corner to the bar.

Chadley is drying the glasses and placing them on one of the four empty trays sitting on top of the counter. She sees me and gives me a nod in greeting as I grab the beers out of the silver double door fridge.

"Do you know when Storm and Aron are coming back?" I've come to know the girl, she's quiet mostly but always seems to know stuff.

"They got back a few minutes ago. Killer left a phone for you, said to tell you he's on speed dial one." She points to the black device on the counter next to where she's standing.

I take the phone and slip it in my pocket.

My eyes widen as I catch the thin strap blue tank she's wearing.

My mouth falls open at the denim shorts that show her ass cheeks for all eyes to see and hands to touch. She notices my ogling but doesn't comment or say anything as she continues with her task.

I look behind me and see the stacks of alcohol packed neatly on to the red wood shelves mounted on the rock styled wall and grab the beer opener hanging from the hook.

Wisp joins us and I'm surprised she is dressed in a long jeans and vest instead of the next to nothing I'm used of seeing her wearing.

"Someone wants to get spanked tonight." Wisp says in a sing song voice, as she walks by us and smacks Chadley playfully on the ass.

She doesn't greet me but I don't care. The girl can't stand me, plain as day.

When Venus or one of the men are around, she tends to say a few words to me for their sake.

But now, with Chadley as the only eyes besides the two of us, there is no false Wisp. What she hopes to do has the opposite effect on me because I prefer the bitchy, but real Wisp any day over the false one.

I take the beer to the two men watching sports and It isn't long that I join in with Chadley getting the bar ready for the mother chapter.

XVIII

"I'm sorry, Okay."

I grab a glass and start drying it up, mindful of the big biker standing just a few feet away. It's now closing on eight and we've just finished with dinner which was from a fast food restaurant called Meaty pizza and doughnuts.

Zero sat next to Falon far away from me pretending I don't exist while he laughed with Falon and Venus over some crap, which was fine by me.

Killer is still a no show but Aron has kept me busy. I spent dinner playing i-spy with him and Storm. I lost most of the time. The kid is cool but doesn't like to lose, he also doesn't like to bath which was fine by me. I wanted to ask Killer but decided he was probably busy.

Aron is with Venus and Texas in Killers room, setting up his PS4 as he calls his PlayStation. He wants me to play with them but I know I'll suck at it so I asked Storm who has agreed to join us.

The past few hours have been Zero free thus far, but he's here now.

"Don't sweat it." I shrug like its nothing and ignore him standing there as I continue to work on tidying up the bar and putting the snacks out.

It'll be a few hours until the Houston Chapter arrive and I meet the mother chapter of the outlaw bikers.

Apparently, I am in for a night I won't forget as Venus explained to me.

The Satan Snipers are 1percenters. They make their own rules and one of them is that The Satan Snipers love open sex.

I'm not surprised, I have been to parties before.

I have an idea of how bad things could get, but I didn't voice any of this to the beautiful woman.

Aron is going to be sleeping by then, hopefully. I'm not sure I like all these guys around the kid, sleeping or not so I need to keep my eyes open tonight.

"Beauty look at me please."

I spin around and stare at his sullen face,

"What do you want Zero?" I sigh, "My name is Beggar, it's not beauty, it's Beggar, okay, I said it was good. We good, we said what we had to say, don't worry about it. How many times are you gonna keep apologizing?"

His face crumbles, and I feel that tug as my resolve slides a fraction.

"Until I stop feeling like shit."

I nod once like I understand then turn back to my job. I don't want him to be here. Why can't he leave me alone? Zero is creeping in my thoughts, slowly stealing my mind a second at a time.

I've done good these last few hours. I haven't thought about him, haven't thought about his promises and kisses, I haven't thought about his ultimatums.

This day with Zero has been a world wind of numerous emotions that are confusing and dangerous.

"Can't we just go for a walk. And talk."

I turn back to him, glad that my hair is tied up and huff,

"No, we can't. I'm working. This job is important to me, Zero. I am a beggar and I'm homeless. I can't go for walks. This is my life you messing with. The Satan Snipers gave me a job. Gave me a chance. People like me don't get chances very often if ever. Please don't ruin it for me, just go away, please."

His eyes widen and I'm not sure what's that look on his face.

Maybe regret maybe something else.

I'm not sure and I shouldn't care.

So, why the hell do I want to know? But I can't that's the problem. He isn't mine.

Zero is Falon's man.

He is going to marry her. He should marry her. This feeling for me, it'll fade, it has to.

He walks closer to me and I won't lie, my knees feel like buckling in.

Zero doesn't hold me, or touch me but for the kiss he places on my head.

His lips linger on my hair and I close my eyes.

Why? Why me?

"I'll pick you up after work."

He spins around and leaves before I can say no., I watch his leather covered form GO around the corner thinking what just happened.

My phone rings in my pocket at that very second. I put the glass down and take it out of my jeans already knowing who it is.

"Hello." I snicker at how awful I must sound.

"Hold on a sec." Killer ruffles something while I wait for him.

My back turned to the open space and my eyes trained on the various bottles of alcohol.

"What you up to? got tired of waiting for you to call."

"I didn't know you wanted me to call, I've been waiting for you to call me," I smile but he can't see it.

"Thank my impatience I didn't keep waiting. Where's my nephew at?" Killer asks in a low voice like he doesn't want anyone to hear him. Ha.

"Setting up his PS4 in your room with Texas and Venus, I'm still on my shift."

"Got some stuff I'm busy with, not sure if I'll be back tonight, you think you can sleep with Aron for me. I feel like shit leaving the kid. David is going to shit bricks if he finds out I left his kid at the Clubhouse unattended."

"I was going to anyway but then I heard you don't want to sleep with me anymore."

"What? Who told you that shit? Wait, Zero right."

"Right." I answer, my voice small but still damaged just like my soul.

I've gotten close to Killer; we have a connection that's beyond simple friendship. We understand each other. And unlike Zero who wants to save me, Killer accepts me.

He doesn't ask questions and I don't lie.

He's quiet for a minute and I would put the phone down if it wasn't for his breathing.

"Beggar, I've known the guy for years, and I've never seen Zero lose his shit over any woman. Falon is, what you call it..."

"Perfect." I answer.

"Fuck no, I was going for simple. Zero wants to settle down, she knows the life and won't expect more than he is willing to give her, it's simple. But you, I see the way he watches you, and I see the way you look at him when you think no one notices. The fact that he's willing to break up with a sure thing for a girl who won't even tell him her name is deep stuff Beggar. I think you should stop listening to what is right and what should be and start listening to what you want, and it isn't me you want sleeping next to you."

"Zero put you up to this didn't he?"

He chuckles,

"Give my brother a chance, if you still feel you want me in your bed by the end of the week, I'll gladly come. Now I got shit to do, look after Aron and make sure he baths, kid loves staying dirty."

"Yeah, got it, see you when you get back, alive." I emphasize the last part.

"Yes ma'am." He laughs as I cut the call.

I return to my work, only this time nothing can keep my mind off Zero.

What a foolish man. I don't hold back the smile that tugs on my lips as I finish setting up the counter with snacks.

It's an hour later and finally I'm done for now.

Texas said the others will arrive about midnight so I'm free for the next few hours.

I get to the steps as Aron is walking down.

"Beggar, come on, you said you'll play," He whines, his head tilted to the side again. The boy just can't help being cute.

"I'm comin' kid." I walk faster, two steps at a time. We turn the corner down the hall toward Killer's room.

I get there and stop by the door as Aron runs in, throwing himself on the huge bed.

The light blue duvet is messed and I know he's been jumping on the bed. Another thing Killer told me he can't do.

Texas and Storm are sitting on a square box that resembles a couch in front of the bed immersed in the game.

They don't take their eyes off the big flat screen t.v. that's rooted on the light grey wall.

I make my way next to Aron, watching him stuff his face with popcorn, making even more mess and I sit on the end.

It's clear why the kid loves it here and I feel a twinge in my heart for my baby girl.

She'll be about his age by now. He offers me the bowl of popcorn but I shake my head.

"You gotta bath kid." He has a fistful of popcorn in his little hand that's half way to his open mouth.

His hair is hanging lifelessly to the front of his face and he just freezes.

Then everything happens so fast.

Aron throws the popcorn in my face, jumps off the bed, past Storm and Texas, knocking their drinks down and out the door.

"Aron, not cool," Texas shouts.

I chase after him at the same time big burly hands catch his little body's retreat and lifts him up.

"Uncle Logan put me down." His legs kick out and his body moving like crazy.

My steps falter and I just stand there watching Zero.

He's laughing as he tickles a crazy Aron,

"Are you going to run?"

"No, No, No." Aron laughs, screaming in giggles. He is shaking like crazy. If you looking at them, you'll think the kid might fall but with Zero holding him I know he's safe.

Zero stops his onslaught and ruffles Aron's hair finally noticing me.

The hunger in his eyes undoes me and for the first time in years I want to be touched by a man.

"I thought you left with Falon." I walk closer to him, mindful of the little boy in his arms laughing.

"Nope, sent Den with her in a cage. Heading to Houston tomorrow for a few days."

"Oh," My voice drops. I didn't think he was leaving.

"Come on let's bath this little man."

"I'm not little, I'm big," Aron says.

"Big hey," Zero taunts as he starts lifting a squealing Aron in the air. I stop in front of them, the minty scent from his body does something to me.

He puts Aron down and turns toward his bedroom with Aron in front. The kid runs into Zero's bedroom and I speed up my steps expecting Zero to go in but he surprises me and turns to face me instead. His gaze is brimmed with lust and promise.

His body stopping me mid-step. I gulp and hard.

"Tell me your name!" And just like that I'm dropping my eyes to his chest.

"It's Beggar."

Zero doesn't like my change in mood and cups my cheek in his big hand, using his thumb to lift my chin up.

The other hand is on the wall above my head. His hair is falling to the one side still slightly wet.

A small smile lines his lips, the same lips I've kissed today, the same lips I wish to kiss now.

XIX

I cage her, getting lost in those eyes. The lights in the corridor are dimly lit, giving her a fairy glow.

"Tell me what you feeling." I demand.

"You keep taunting me, controlling me but I'm not yours. Why do I feel you're mine?" Her eyes are so lost. So fucking lost.

She doesn't have a clue.

I rest my chin on her forehead,

"You are mine Beauty, your body has been telling you it from day one, your mind just hasn't caught up yet."

"Uncle Logan and Beggar sitting in the tree k.i.s.s.i.n.g ." Aron sings, his head popping in and out breaking our moment.

Beggar's hand to my chest gives me slight push. I take a hesitant, a very hesitant and slow step back from her.

And I can't help the laugh that bubbles up in me when she practically runs into my room.

Even the boy thinks it's funny.

I want to go in there with them but the raging hard on I got isn't going to go away if I do.

I trek to the opposite end. Storm and Texas are cleaning up Killers room. It's in a fucking state.

"He is going to fuck y'all up when he gets back," I chuckle as I walk in.

"Good thing I'm the VP, this ones on you Tex." Storm chortles as he picks up the empty cans riddled on the floor.

"Ya think he gonna give a fuck 'bout that, blame the kid." Texas drawls from the opposite side of the bed.

Storm throws the beer cans in the empty bin,

"Remind me again why the fuck we are scared of him? He's a kid."

"A kid that can kill you with fucking toilet paper," I say.

It's obvious.

We all quieten and stare at the room. Texas has the duvet in his hands, Storm is holding the popcorn bowl and me I'm just standing there with my arms crossed and we all think the same fucking thing.

"We need the women!" We all say it together.

Texas and Storm go down in search of the girls while I head back to check on Beggar.

I hear the two of them in the bathroom. The shower is running and the door is a jar. Beggar's ass faces the door as she scrubs the kid who is singing some whacky song.

I lean against the frame of my bathroom door enjoying the show. It all looks good.

She's enjoying herself. I notice how she likes taking care of people.

She's always helping, keeping busy. What she doesn't know is that she's shit at washing dishes.

Knight and Spade have been redoing the dishes at night when she's asleep.

"Can you help me out, I need to get his clothes from my room." Her voice is small, when she faces me and my gut tells me I'm missing something.

I wait for her to leave the bathroom. Then I take the towel and throw it at him, "Hope you enjoyed that, 'cause you just earned time out by the wall," I tell him.

Aron is naughty and he should be bathing himself but with David for a dad and Beggar at his beck and call I don't blame him.

After ten minutes, and a naked, sleepy Aron I know Beggar isn't coming. I go to my cupboard and fetch one of Falon's t-shirts and slip it on the kid. By the time I'm tucking him in he is out for the count.

It takes me half hour to find Venus and get her to watch the kid while I look for Beggar.

By eleven I'm walking toward the lake, blanket in hand. It's a trek.

I pass the stables and the barn heading toward the small hill. Why Beggar likes to come this side is a mystery. It's dark and creepy.

The other women would never come here at night but then again isn't it why I call her Beauty. I wish she'll just tell me her name.

Trust is a hard thing for me and with Beggar it's harder. She has so much secrets, so many nightmares and I want to know her. I need to.

By the time I make it to the hill, it's drizzling. I walk closer to her form. She's in the rain in a thin strap vest and hasn't moved an inch. Lost in her mind.

What does she think about? Is she thinking about the man she says owns her? I wasn't lying when I told her I'll kill him. I will.

I'm at the end of patience with waiting, I want her, I need her. I've never wanted a woman so much before. I've never had to work so hard to get a woman to want me either.

Since I've met her, I watched her play with her life as she throws herself on the ground, belittling who she is.

Why does she do it? Why does she deny what it is we have? How can I help her? What do I do?

It's all those questions that remain unanswered as I finally get to her. I wrap the blanket around her shoulders and sit my ass down beside her as my arm pulls her toward my chest.

She fights me and my heart aches at how broken she is. If I were a lesser man I would have broken down and cried.

"It's only me." She settles at my voice. Her head resting on my chest.

There is no moon to light our darkness as we watch the tears from the sky feed the lake. My hold on her tightens at just the thought of tomorrow. I'll have to leave her here. I have to go hunt Jade down, and kill the guys who took her.

I'll return with more blood on my hands, more lives I've taken. She must sense my distress 'cause I feel the heat of her lips as she places a soft kiss to my chest.

She lifts her eyes to me and it's so dark I can't see her, but I feel her lips on my neck,

"Claim me Zero, show me what it is to be yours."

"Not here, come on." I plant a chaste kiss on her nose before I help her up.

Her hand finds mine and our fingers link. I pull her in a partial run and she laughs whenever she almost stumbles as we move up the hill, back to where we came.

By the time we get to the kitchen door we are soaked.

Her hair is plastered to her arms and neck. Her nipples pebbled into small points.

I look into her eyes, her need, her want for me so strong that I shake to restrain myself from taking her right here, up against the back door.

It's in this moment staring at my own black beauty that I'm a man.

I'm not the Enforcer, I'm just a man who is about to claim his woman.

She opens the kitchen door for us to enter and I watch her body move like a man hypnotized as we walk up the stairs so silently. I don't even hear my brothers or anyone for that matter.

It's like a never-ending trance until I hear the click of the door.

My hands wrap around her waist. One curves to the shape of her form, the other goes straight for her pussy.

Her neck tilts as she moans. I pull her ass closer, grinding my cock against her at the same time my four fingers apply pressure to her hot pussy, rubbing leisurely up and down.

Her body is so responsive, it's almost like she's not the same girl.

But those raspy throaty sounds she's making assures me it's her.

She spins around and takes a step back, and I watch the inner battle she has with herself.

I don't move or hide from her. I want this, I want my cock so deep in her pussy that she'll never want for another man but she has to want it too.

She has to want me enough to fight that mind of hers and win.

"I need our first time to be with the lights off."

I go to retort but I stop.

I'll have enough time to explore her body with my eyes in the future. Today I'll learn her body with my hands.

I flip the light switch, shutting us in darkness. Her silhouette moves closer to me, we both slip our wet t-shirts off.

Her calloused fingers start from my neck to my collar bone, grazing my nipples as they map their way over pectorals and down over my leathers.

I hiss.

My cock jumps, needing to be released.

"Beauty." I say as a warning.

"Kiss me Zero."

I do just that.

I grab her naked waist and crush her breast to my chest. Something seals between us and I swear we are soul mates.

I pull her wet hair out of her face; grab the back of her neck and fuse our mouths together. She kisses me as hungry as I kiss her and we don't stop. I've never had a woman who can kiss like her. She's perfect.

My hands explore her naked flesh, learning her body with my fingers. From the dip in her spine to the raised skin just below her left shoulder.

I don't need my fingers to know the burn that's branded her torso or the fullness of her breast. I grab at her ass squeezing it through the wet jeans. Her moans fill the room as her greedy fingers tug on my belt and I stop kissing her. A hum leaves my throat as our mouth part.

"Strip, I need inside you now."

I hear her low laugh as I unbuckle my pants. The chains from my wallet hit the carpeted floor with a loud thud.

My cock springs free, high and proud.

I play with the tip to give him some attention as he waits for Beggar to take off her jeans. She lays down on the bed waiting for me. I see the shape of her form, her knees bent up. My hands work faster.

I could come by just this.

The wetness that leaks from the tip of my cock to my fingers remind me that I don't have a condom.

"Fuck!" I squeeze the tip of my cock, my jaw tight, mouth in a firm line.

"What's wrong, don't tell me you changed your mind." I chuckle at the sound of her frustration, make light of my painful cock.

"Fuck no."

"Then what?"

"I need a condom." *Shit.*

"Don't be mad, but, ah, Killer put a box in the draw."

I swear my cock gets softer hearing that and any logical sense I have slips away, dying a quick death.

I stalk toward her, and grip her ankles the way I had earlier. My hands explore the back of her legs right up to her thighs until it reaches so close to her heat.

I part her legs, letting the cool air hit her naked heat.

She moans.

My mouth finds her wet shaved pussy. I give it a long lick, then I start sucking. I work her body up with only my mouth, my tongue.

When she tries to close her legs, I nip her swollen lips. I don't put my fingers inside her.

She wants to be claimed, I want to claim her and that's exactly what I'm going to do.

When I feel her get wetter, I climb over her, line my cock to her pussy and I slam home. She cries out in bliss, and I'm sure pain. Her walls clench around me from the intrusion.

I still when I really just want to move. I kiss her lightly sheen forehead, cheeks and eyes.

"You are so beautiful!" Our tongues tangle in a lover's embrace, leisurely, just happy to be together.

Her waist lifts in a silent plea for more and I'm glad because I'm not fully in. She's too tight.

I withdraw almost all the way out and slam in harder until I'm balls deep. The noises from her throat are too much even for me. She's expecting me to go fast, expecting me to hammer into her and I want to do just that. I shock us both when I cage her in with my elbows on either side of her face and I rock into her slow and deep.

I kiss her nose as her hands go to my back. Her blunt fingers making futile attempts to grip into my slippery flesh and for the first time I make love to Beggar.

I don't stop my slow burning rhythm until she arches up, silent and beautiful as her body gives me everything in that orgasm.

Her walls clench impossibly tight around my cock, pulsing, sucking me deeper into a crescendo of unattainable heights that I have no choice but to spill my seed deep in her womb.

I know my cock isn't softening soon and I don't want to leave her warmth just yet. I grab Beggar by the waist and roll back, so my dick doesn't slip out.

"What are you doing?" Her knees are on either side of my hips and her chest comes down to mine. I bend my chin to look at her even though it's dark.

"Getting comfortable, that was a taster, claiming you is going to take a while." I feel for the lamp switch next to the bed at the same time she sits up on me. Her eyes widen.

She goes to cover her stomach but I pull her hands away.

"I've already seen it, there's no reason to hide."

Her eyes take on a haunting look before she gives me a sharp nod and then bends back down to lay on my chest.

I play with her hair, knowing she's lost in her mind again. I'm just glad she's with me, that we've shared this together.

"When I was younger, I was a beggar by circumstance, when I got older, I remained a beggar by choice."

I stiffen but I don't say a word.

"I never had an easy life Zero. My mother died when I was 12. I got shoved into the system and dumped off at a foster home with 8 other kids.

My foster father raped me 2 weeks later. I killed him with a tin opener and took my chances on the streets.

It wasn't too bad 'cause I've lived there my whole life. I never went back to school and I never did anything too dangerous. I stuck to the bins and kept the begging to a minimum. But a few years later I wanted something better, I knew I couldn't live like that forever, so I looked for my father. I waited for him one day outside some fancy restaurant.

I was so hungry and almost went inside to see where he was and if he'll give me some food but I didn't. When I finally approached him, he laughed in my face.

When I told him my mother's name, he put a gun to my head. He said I was a liar. He didn't believe I was his kid, he said she died years ago. He said if he ever saw me again, he'll put a bullet in my head. After that day I lost hope until I met Patricia, she was a prostitute, said that if I went to this one club, I could get a job waitressing or something, but I had to get an I.D card. It took me weeks to get one, I was sixteen, they didn't hire younger than eighteen. I was fucked, I used all my money on that card.

That's the day I met him.

I was just a homeless girl and he was so much more. His name is Lucca and he has your women."

XX

"here the fuck is he?" I growl to myself as I pass Texas and Bull playing pool down the hall.

"Den and Falon was attacked, someone hit them off the road and knocked Den out, took Falon."

Texas curses, putting the pool stick down.

"Gotta get the women on lock down and fast. I'll call After, see if she can gather up the rest of the women in a cage and bring them down." Texas storms out already on the phone.

I look at the lone brother standing on the other end of the pool room, he's sober today, and I respect him even more.

He knows shit is going down so he has put his own needs last. My father is the President of our mother chapter in Houston. Why he insisted I become the VP of this chapter only he knows.

Most of the time it's a shit load of work and not many rewards. My time isn't my own, but there are few moments like this, when I see the reward. My brothers got my back.

"You look good today brother," I tell Bull. He grunts a reply before his phone reaches his ear.

Texas marches back in, "After said she'll handle it, will be here a sap."

"Zero is going to take this shit bad, have you guys seen him?" I ask.

Texas frowns, "What the fuck you talkin' bout."

I sigh, I didn't want them to find out like this, but fuck it I'm the VP.

"Zero is going to claim Falon."

"I think you got your shit mixed up, he's with Beggar. I saw them with my own eyes. They've been upstairs for a while now, he ain't claimin' no Pritzy Princess."

My anger boils, what the fuck is he doing with Beggar. The girl is just getting her footing.

Shit.

I can't believe he'll use Beggar like that. I didn't see this shit happening, I presumed she was with Killer. This isn't good.

I don't say shit to Texas. I'm already halfway up the stairs. My phone rings, I pull it out from my jeans, 'blocked number.'

I have no intention to answer it, so I hold it in my hand letting it ring off as I go to Beggar's room door. My fist pounds on the wood until it's pulled open.

Zero's glare eases when he sees me. Who was he expecting?

The sex is thick in the air.

They have been here for a while. I look behind the snarly man and when I'm sure Beggar isn't in hearing range. I push his naked chest.

"What the hell are you thinking?"

He looks behind him, and then he steps out as I step back and closes the door.

"I was going to talk to you about it but it happened so fast."

I see the look in his eyes and I groan.

He's in love with Beggar, fuck.

I sucker punch him in the stomach.

He grumbles as he weaves, "What the fuck!"

"You know I had to do that, she's one of us. Don't fuck it up, she doesn't need any more shit in her life."

"You think I don't know that, huh, I'm a grown ass man."

"Yeah, I hear you brother. But I gotta tell you something and you ain't gonna like it."

Zero straightens, his finger playing with his scar.

"What?"

"Falon's been jacked." He punches the wall.

"Fuck," He yells.

The constant noise of my phone starts to annoy me and I answer the blocked call.

"Who the hell is this?" I bark.

The voice on the other end laughs, and I have a bad feeling about this. I look to Zero, signaling him to get a tracker on the caller. He runs into his room next door, all the while I listen to the laughing voice.

"Is that anyway to greet the person who has your women?" His Italian accent thick. That voice, a hard one to forget.

"Sanati. How long were you plotting your revenge, it's been years, why now? Jade, I can understand, but why did you take Falon, she did nothin' to you."

He laughs, "Revenge? You think I did all this for revenge, I am not a fool Mr Radley. You think I'll go to war with a group of trained snipers for the death of measly soldiers." He bellows like it's a ridiculous idea.

"Then what the fuck are you doing with our women."

"Insurance. It has come to my attention you have something I'm looking for, something that is mine. I want it, no I need it back. You get your precious ladies back and I get what I want, win, win. So, when should we trade?"

"Trade what?"

He chuckles and it's starting to annoy me, "Both your girls for mine."

"What the hell? We got no girl of yours."

"But you do, you found her in Washington a week ago. She probably told you her name is Beggar." I freeze.

My answer?

Silence.

"Ah, so you do know her after all. She's mine. I would like her back, please."

"No." I grip the phone tighter.

"Excuse me?"

"I said no, she isn't yours. You the one that raped her aren't you motherfucker."

"My relationship with her is between the two of us, now I do not appreciate you assuming things that you do not understand."

"Then explain it to me."

"No, please let Beggar know that I miss her dearly, and that she has one hour to call me. Oh, and If she refuses to return to me by Wednesday, the deal will be off and your poor woman will be minced for my dogs that's after my soldiers are done with them of course."

The line goes dead.

I charge into Zero's room but stop short when I see Venus and Aron fast asleep on the bed. Zero is on the floor, laptop on his lap. I walk slowly toward him and tap his shoulder signaling him to meet me outside.

XXI

I pace up and down the corridor, my bare feet taking up the long stretch of space in quick strides.

Texas, Spade, Storm, Bull and Zero have been in my room for an hour, they have their cuts on so I know this is bad. It's close to one in the morning.

The Houston chapter will be arriving at the Clubhouse in the next half hour.

I have no clue what's going on besides that Lucca has called.

When Aron told me earlier, he heard Killer telling his dad that Jade was missing, I made a call to someone who could find information to help them.

I didn't think that the information will be Lucca.

He actually kidnapped her.

The bedroom door opens and Zero steps out.

"Come on Beauty," I follow him inside the room.

Spade is the first face I see, and he looks livid as he leans against the window. His arms cross over his chest as he glares at me from across the room.

Texas is plastered to the chair in front of the bed, his face in a bored mask. But he isn't fooling anyone.

I'm startled forward at the fingers on my back. Thank god I'm wearing long jeans and a t-shirt because my hair isn't going to protect me from these angry bikers.

I feel Zero's presence behind me but I don't turn around. I look to the man sitting on the bed. And right now, he isn't my friend he is the Vice President of The Satan Sniper's Motorcycle Club and I'm the threat.

I swallow some phlegm that comes up from the back of my throat.

"I'll tell you what you want to know, but my name is my own." I say it to all of them but my eyes stay on Storm.

"You got no fucking choice," Spade retorts.

Zero is across the room in seconds and has Spade in a chokehold as Texas shouts,

"Don't talk to her like that."

I'm standing in the middle of the space watching it all unfold.

How did Lucca find me so quickly?

My contact said one of the men had to be working for Lucca. My first thought was Knight, but Knight is part of the Famiglia.

The Famiglia are enemies of the New Orleans outfit.

"Zero let him go brother. We just talkin', no one is going to hurt Beggar and Spade keep your mouth shut. I'm the one in charge here, so everyone sit the fuck down. We have two women to find, Beggar sit down please."

Zero keeps his position for a few seconds longer before he lets Spade go. They do some handshake arm thing and they're cool. *Men.*

I take my place on the bed, until my back hits the headboard.

Knees to my chest, hands to my toes, chin to my knees, but it doesn't touch. It mustn't.

My hair doesn't fall properly over my face to hide me, but I'm okay. I have an Enforcer in the room to save me.

The room quietens and I don't look at any of them. My eyes stay firmly on my white bedding.

"Let's start with the basic question, how do you know Lucca Sanati?"

I hear that name of his and my mind goes instantly back to the day we met, when I was just a girl and he was so much more.

"My mother had been dead for four years. I ran away from the system at twelve after the man who was assigned to look after me, raped me. It was hard to survive on my own. I was sixteen, cold, hungry and stupid when I met Lucca. I wanted to get a job. Get a life. This girl I met told me I had to look in this club, she said they'd hook me up if I got an I.D card."

"What kind of job girly girl?" The question comes from Knight.

I didn't hear him enter the room. Still, I answer.

"I wasn't looking to be a prostitute if that's what you asking. I was thinking more of a waiter. I was stupid, I got the I.D not realizing that I had to be eighteen to work there. Got turned down before I even entered. I was hungry and so tired that day. I had to walk 10 blocks for that gig. I just sat there, outside this joint. It was closing on 10 that night when I saw him jumping out of his black Bentley. He was so handsome in his black suit, his smile so big."

A throat clears, snapping me out of the daze that is my mind.

"He took me out to some fancy ass place but the kitchen was closed so we ate cold sandwiches. It was nice. He was nice. After that I met him every few days. We dated until the night I was due to move in with him, he found my I.D card in my back pocket..."

I shake my head as memories of that day claw its way to the forefront of my mind. My reality slipping.

"Im going to fuckin' kill you," His angry voice hisses in my ear.

My screaming is so loud as he pulls my hair. The brutal punch he delivers to my stomach, I feel it all. The loss of air, my wheezing chest as I try to regain the loss of oxygen. I remember thinking I was going to die.

"No, no, no, no, please, please, I beg you. I don't wanna talk anymore about this please." My fingers lock around my toes until my knuckles are white as I fight off my nightmares.

I rock myself back and forth, my chin doesn't touch my knees. It mustn't.

"He got Jade, took Falon a few hours ago. He wants a trade Beauty." Zero says in a small and haunting voice.

A phone chimes cutting off any further talking. Storm answers it and grunts.

"He wants to talk to you, no speaker." My head shoots up to Storm who looks remorseful as he holds the phone for me to take. I swallow the memories that cloud my mind.

Memories of *him*.

And I take the phone putting it to my ear.

"Beggar, Beggar, Beggar, my filthy dirty Beggar." He laughs at his own sick joke.

"Lucca." My accent thick as my memories fight for my mind.

He knows, he can tell.

"ENOUGH!" He commands and my mind instantly obeys like the obedient slave I was trained to be.

"You costed me a lot of money and a lot of men Amariya, millions. I'm tempted to take it out on the red head. She's so tiny, easy breakable, but all will be forgotten if you give me one thing."

"What do you want Lucca?" I stammer like a little girl.

I hate how scared I am of him.

I hate him!

What he did to me!

What he took from me!

"You know full well what I fucking want. I want my daughter," He says it likes it's the most obvious thing in the world.

"I told you, she's dead," I whisper but my voice is firm.

He laughs.

He always laughs.

"You lie, you always lie Amariya, it was the biggest problem with you. I know you got her somewhere, it's only a matter of time until I find out where."

"I won't lie about this Lucca. I wish it was a fucking lie, I wish I had her." I scream, "but you, you took her from me. You raped me! You took what I would've given you for free, what I gave you for free, so YOU killed her, not me."

"It was consensual, you SIGNED the contract." He shouts and I swear if he was here, he would've strangled me.

"I was sixteen, what the fuck did I know about signing contracts? I trusted you! It was you who left me with those men, you told them to take me back. Do you know what they did to me? YOUR. MEN. Your loyal fucking servants. DO YOU?" I scream, and snarl.

He's silent and normally I would keep quiet. But no more.

For the first time in four years I tell Lucca exactly what I have to.

"They left me in a god damn ditch for two days. My voice is fucked from screaming. Do you know I didn't even have it checked out, huh! Let's not forget the week I walked around naked without clothes, begging with a cardboard box on. And the days I went without food, without water." I laugh but it's hollow just like my soul.

Shaking my head, I say, "You wouldn't understand the idea of being hungry, or the reality of it if you're pregnant, but I'll explain it to you, our daughter didn't stand a chance."

He's quiet, and for a second I swear I hear him breakdown but he clips the phone off, so I guess I'll never know.

I look up at the men, there's like twenty different men in the room and Venus looking at me with shocked expressions, except Zero because he already knows.

I didn't tell him everything but I told him what was important.

He didn't take it very well but he hid it well.

I hand Storm back his phone and regain my position.

"I need to make a phone call. He'll be here soon."

They all move aside as I climb off the bed. Everyone is silent.

These new people must think I'm crazy. They just walked in, and the first thing they saw was one of my episodes.

Maybe I am crazy.

But I'm the best and only hope they have of getting Jade and Falon back.

I walk out of the lounge and go to the front door, aware Zero is behind me. I dial up the only person I've never doubted.

The person I met when I was sixteen and pregnant, he was my last hope and he never failed.

The price I paid was worth it.

A life for a life. *Una vita per una vita.*

"Talk." The bark of his voice makes me smile even in my darkest of moments.

"We spoke about that, it's mean."

He's quiet for a long minute,

"Fuck you Riya, where the fuck are you? You just vanished overnight."

"Nice to hear your voice too Boss man, but this isn't social."

"We're Italian and family of course it's social."

My voice drops,

"Lucca called. He seems to think our daughter survived."

"Fuck," I hear him throw something.

He never could control his temper.

"I was thinking the same thing. He's coming here, I know it, he won't wait until Wednesday."

He knows what I'm talking about, why I'm saying what I'm saying, but only him.

"I'll bring your stuff."

"That's exactly what I wanted to hear."

"But, I don't fucking like it, this is the last time Riya, that Strunzo better be clipped by next week or I'm sending Vince with a Moe Green Special."

I shake my head, "See you soon Boss man."

I clip the phone off and face Zero's tired gaze.

"Come on, you need to sleep. Falon will be fine."

He pulls me in closer as his hands squeeze my ass.

"You damn well know it's not Falon I'm worried about."

I kiss his cheek, "And you damn well know I have to do this. I know Lucca, he doesn't make empty threats and his men won't stop at just killing your men. They'll hunt your family down, rape your children and burn your houses, this isn't a war ground with rules Zero, this is the outfit, there is no fucking rules."

I push away from his warmth and walk past him, no doubt he's following. He's always following me.

"Beauty, whatever you thinking about doing don't. We've hardly had anytime. We haven't even really spoken."

When I'm silent, he shakes his head.

"I planned to tell you this over dinner or a picnic or some romantic shit like that, not like this."

I frown, "What are you talking about?"

His shoulders slump, "I'm being deployed."

I stop dead in my tracks.

"It's a covert operation, I got two weeks with you, don't cut it short by going to that motherfucker, please stay, give us a chance."

My stomach sinks and for the first time since I met Zero, I do the very thing that he warned me not to- I lie to his face.

"Ok, I won't go until I really have to."

The relief is evident as his shoulders drop. I smile at him, and it's not a hard thing to do. He looks dangerous and sexy in his cut and chains hanging from his pants, a true badass biker.

Taking the few steps toward him I place a chaste kiss to his cheek. My back turns, missing the disappointment that marks his face.

I don't bother with the new bikers that are lurking in the house with half naked girls hanging off their arms.

I don't look up when a cloud of smoke blows in my face. I keep my gaze to the floor, inhaling the thick smell of beer and stale smoke now masking the strong disinfectant that normally fills the air in this area.

Zero's voice rings from me behind me as he stops to greet his brothers. I'm glad he has them here with him. He'll need them soon.

If there is one thing about Lucca I know is, he will never let me go.

I'm not the least bit surprised when my phone chimes as I enter my room. I don't have to question how he got the number. Someone is working for him.

The Satan Snipers have a rat, and I know the Enforcer will hunt them down.

"Amariya, Il mio mendicante."

"Not anymore, give them back their women Lucca." I sigh, but inside I'm dying a thousand deaths. Hearing his voice, seeing him is the one thing I never want to do ever again.

But since my conversation with him earlier I feel so much stronger. I have to be if I'm going to kill him.

He ignores me, "Do you remember that job you did for your dear old cousin." I stiffen mid-way to the bed mindful of the door opening behind me.

I know it's Zero when his hands wrap around my waist.

"I'm not sure what you talking about Lucca," I say his name out loud for Zero's benefit.

"Oh, let me refresh your memory, two in the head, one in the back, you filthy, dirty, beggar. Remember that?" He chuckles but it's different from before, like it's almost forced.

"You mean your goons that tried to steal me for you." I'm not going to like what he has to say, I know it. I never had.

He laughs, "They were hardly goons, one was a P.I remember him, ring any bells, the white Texas man." It's the face I had trouble remembering.

I step out of Zero's arms putting distance between us.

"You lying, no it can't be." Even my voice sounds doubtful.

"Oh yes yes yes yes yes yes, say hello to your boyfriend for me will you." He laughs as the call goes dead.

I'm still frowning when I face Zero, who's slipping his cut off his shoulders and placing it like a priceless gem on the chair that Texas left in front of the bed.

"Can you tell me about your family, do you have brothers or sisters?"

If he is shocked by my sudden question, he doesn't show it.

He proceeds to the bed, sitting down to untie his boots.

"My dad is on his way from Seattle, had some club stuff to sort out, but we can see him tomorrow. My brother is in a rehab facility, got stabbed in the back, doctors said he'll never walk again but the man is persistent. He'll be home in a month. My mother is dead to me, haven't seen her since I was a kid, the rest we can talk 'bout another time, maybe tomorrow."

He stands up sliding out of his pants and turns to face me.

"Gotta head out in the morning. Tonight, I just need to hold you, please. I know you don't like to be touched and shit when you sleep, please Beauty, just tonight."

His voice breaks and I run into his arms.

"You can hold me every night."

He lifts me up, my legs wrap around his waist.

"Every night ha?" His voice drops into a sexy growl causing my sensitive pussy to clench. His eyes take on that bedroom look he does sometimes where the one gets smaller. The scar under the eye is something I wanna know about him. But I don't ask, as he said we will have other nights.

Even as the thought leaves me, a sense of foreboding settles within me.

"Kiss me." I tell him, desperation stark in my voice as need to feel this man in me, claiming me over and over again becomes a suffocating fuse burning to be set free, screaming to be fulfilled.

He groans, as he licks his lips and does just that.

He consumes me with a kiss of contentment, a kiss of hunger, a kiss of pain.

He strips my clothes the same way he strips my soul with each touch of his hands, each dig of his fingers as he claims my flesh, unraveling me until all I can do is feel.

And I feel everything, the glide of his lips as he paints my body with the heat of his breath, awakening my senses, pulling me in until I'm arching up, as the chains of another draws me back.

I writhe and twist under his exploring lips and caging hands.

I cry out as he fills me with all that is him, chest to chest, heart to heart, we collide as one.

Thrust after thrust Zero takes me, claims me, owns me until I have no choice but to pull at the chains that hold me.

I have no choice but to give him the last shred of my humanity, the final piece of me.

XXII

I'm awoken by Beggar screaming, my head pounding.

The bed dips as I turn to grab her by the waist, she obviously fights me but I easily pull her to my chest.

"Stay still," I snap.

She listens, whimpering as her body stills.

"Sleep Beauty," and she does.

It's the first night I sleep with Beggar in my arms. And though I feel her closeness, I know she's safe, there's nothing but a painful ache in my chest at the thought of her going back to that man.

He did this to her, yet she's prepared to relive his torture to protect two girls who would never do the same for her.

She hasn't said it, but her eyes say more.

I know she's going to leave.

I feel it.

She might've been a beggar when she walked into this Clubhouse but now, she's a beggar stealing pieces of me that I'd never knew existed.

She's stealing my heart and I want her to take it. Take it all. The rest will come later.

It's hours later when I get up. Beggar is still fast asleep and I have tons of shit to do besides going to tell the entire club that my woman is the reason Falon and Jade are missing.

I should get out of bed and get on the road. Instead I just watch her sleep. And I notice things I've never noticed before, the faint dust of freckles on her nose, the tiny scar on her temple from an old wound, the light crinkles under her eyes from lack of sleep.

I see how her hair fans out on the pillow. The downward tilt of her lips.

She's beautiful, and so strong.

When she told me about the pregnancy, it was too much. I couldn't fucking deal. I couldn't do it.

I told her I was going to take a piss, but I fucking hurled my guts out.

How did she survive a life like hers? Living on the streets had to be hard, but being subjected to some sick bastard with a fetish of raping women?

Getting raped by numerous men on top of that. Then getting left in a ditch while you're pregnant.

It's almost impossible to believe. Yet, she has the scars, brands and these gut wrenching, mind fucking nightmares to prove it.

Lord knows what other fucked up shit happened to her. At least she's safe now, in my clutches.

I won't let her go now, no way.

"THEN HE CALLED YESTERDAY sayin' she's his, the guy is a sick fuck and that girl has already gone through more shit than all of us put together. There's no way I'm letting her near that fucker." Storm's grim eyes dare any fucker to challenge him.

All the brothers are sitting around the table eating breakfast.

Rounder is at the head of the table, not much better than yesterday, and now his girl is gone.

It is my job to protect her and I failed.

I know I should've taken her to Barfa but fuck, I can't regret that time I spent with Beggar.

And the fact that I'm not losing my shit just confirms what I already knew. My nameless beggar is it for me.

When I took her again last night, fuck, it was something.

I feel a hard on coming just from the thought of her rolled back eyes and parted lips as her body convulsed in the pleasure, I fed her.

A real fucking siren, shit.

I was reluctant to leave her with the women and Prospects who were all ordered to eat in the lounge, so the brothers can discuss the situation.

Venus already agreed to stay with the women and catch up during church later. The two other full members, After and Mercy are on the way with the rest of the women and children from Houston.

Storm just about finishes with a quick rundown of his plan when Den rushes in.

"Sorry, Prez but you guys gotta come see this." His bug eyes tell me I'm not going to like whatever 'this' is.

I'm the first one out my chair, slipping my cut on as I follow the Prospect to the front door. The sun hits me full in the face.

I step out onto the porch spotting the black Bentley and three Mercedes parked outside the gates.

The first person comes to mind is Lucca, he has come for my woman but that thought is squashed when I see an unmistakable face.

All the brothers come join me outside on the porch. Our eyes trained on the cages.

So, I don't spot Beggar until I see her ass climbing down the stairs.

I naturally go after her.

My arm snaps open and I grab her around the waist,

"Where the fuck do you think you going? That's Deno Catelli," I growl into her ear.

"They here for me, I won't be long." She says matter of factly.

"That's the future head of the Mafia.." I remind her, in case she thinks it's Lucca.

"She already knows that, Deno is her family," Killer says from beside her.

I hear the men behind me swear and curse.

My woman just keeps bringing on the surprises, but it answers one question.

Why she chose to be a beggar when she got older. It has been nagging me since last night.

She's protecting her family, like she's protecting us.

Everybody knows the New Orleans Outfit is the biggest enemy of the Famiglia.

One of the brothers open the gates for the cars to drive inside.

They park in a straight line, not too close to the porch.

They lucky we got a big yard.

The sleek two hundred grand cars are completely out of place with the vast number of bikes lined up to the sides.

First the driver and the soldiers step out of the cars.

Three from the back Mercedes and four from the front. All the men are wearing black from the sun glasses, to the suits they are straightening.

It's the men that step out from the two cars in the middle that got my attention.

The blonde headed guy with the light beige suit and white shirt is a familiar. Vincent Stone. He is Killers half-brother from his father's short affair with Vincent's Italian mother.

Beggar struggles to leave my warmth.

And I don't want to let her go as I release her from the safety of my arms.

I follow behind her, but not too close. No way am I letting her get near them alone, family or not.

Killer goes straight to the man in the beige suit and punches him solid in the stomach. The guy barely flinches.

It's those seconds when I take my eyes off Beggar, does she run into Deno's arms.

I walk closer to the Mafia sizing him up.

He has on a dark charcoal suit with a light blue shirt. Out of all the guys in his circle he is the most under dressed. The deadliest too.

Deno has a reputation that's simple, no one fucks with him and lives to speak his name.

I watch his hazel eyes crinkle as he tugs on Beggar's hair. She swats him away like a naughty child.

Why is she so care free with him?!

Jealousy has many ugly heads, men fought wars, lost their lives, killed their brothers because of that one feeling. The fucked-up part about it is, you just can't fucking help it.

I tell myself he is her damn family. I shouldn't be getting pissed off. But I can't help it as I feel myself losing control.

I hardly had anytime with Beggar, we've barely spoken. Normally people get to know each other before things progress, with us it's the opposite.

We jumped right into the sack, before we learnt the comfort of holding hands.

But since I've met Beggar nothing about her is normal, easy. Nothing about this deep need I feel for her is normal either.

Then this guy comes and she's smiling at him like he holds the keys to the moon, and she looks so fucking beautiful.

I wish she smiled at me like that. I clench my fist to my side, grinding my teeth together.

Killer must sense the tension because his eyes find mine and he gives me a chin lift. Letting me know he has her back.

I get the fuck out of there.

My boots cover the distance to the porch, where my brothers are waiting with grim faces.

I don't keep eye contact with any of them.

The few pats on my back does help calm me somewhat.

It ain't easy when a brother has a new woman. It's a hell of a lot less when you don't even know her name.

Most of these guys know how it is. Me? I've never had a relationship before Falon. Growing up as a biker then joining the navy didn't allow me the time to have one.

My dad made me Prospect for a full year before I got patched in. By then I was too busy going to fucking war than to have time for dating.

So it isn't a surprise when I say that I never dated a non-biker girl before Beggar.

Texas taps his hat as I pass him to go into the Clubhouse. I don't need to look at the brother to know he's keeping his eye on Killer and Beggar.

A few minutes later I'm in the kitchen preparing food for Aron.

It's my day to cook, but Venus and Chadley handled the breakfast this morning since there is close to 40 bikers in the Clubhouse.

Good thing too, Chadley is an excellent cook, she runs The Pritz Corner, the club's restaurant here in Kanla and will work in the nightclub once we open doors next month.

She's also an emotional person, so when she's in a mood, no food, no baking, nothing. And Chadley is going to be a wreck once we tell the women later today about Jade and Fal.

We'll have to be stupid to think we can keep this tight lipped. Wisp will figure shit out soon enough, she always does and she won't be quiet about it.

After and Mercy are already in the know but they've known all along.

I watch the omelet simmer.

The vibration from my pocket accompanied by the mute tone puts a smile to my face.

I switch off the stove and slip my iPhone out.

"What happened? Nurse MacDicksy ain't doing it for you anymore? Or did you just fuck the dick outa her?"

The deep laugh on the other end is enough to make my entire fuckin' week.

"Ha, ha. How's my baby bro doin', still fucking old Prez's daughter."

Thorn, my only blood brother has busted my balls from the time I told him about Falon.

He thought me dating her was the funniest thing I've ever done. I didn't bust his nuts only because he was paralyzed after some pussy stabbed him in the back a few years ago.

He wasn't sure who pushed the metal in his spine. Just that it was in Washington D.C and he was there for a pick up. It was hard to get revenge or find anything.

I looked for the first year, the whole club did but even with contacts I kept ending up with nothing.

The blue bloods just wanted the case closed and made a dead kid the prime suspect.

The evidence was reclusive.

I believe it was a professional job and I always suspected my brother knew more than he shared.

Which was what motivated him to get better, and the only reason why I never called him on it.

It's a no brainer that he will seek revenge.

Unlike my dad and I who live and breathe the club my bro decided to venture on his own after he left the Air Force.

He started off as a bounty hunter and after a few short years and a fuck load of money, he opened an A-list Personal Investigation company.

I'm fucking proud to have him as my brother. I've always looked up to him growing up, he was my hero.

He practically raised me after mom left, not one day did he complain.

He asked me to join him years ago, but I always knew that I'll end up with the club.

My brother knew it too, because he never asked me again.

"Nah man, I gotta new woman, she's definitely the one, her names Beauty, can't wait for you to hurry your ass up and meet her," I say.

He's so silent I look at my screen to make sure he hasn't cut the call.

"Serious? You shitting me," He laughs, and I know it's real, it's always real when Thorn laughs, "Jesus, she must be a fucking nun to have you dumping Falon's ass. I bet she isn't too happy about that."

I flinch, and I'm glad he can't see me do it.

"I haven't told her yet, was waiting for her to get back from Barfa and break things down gently, but there's some shit happening with the club and Beauty is in the middle of it."

I don't elaborate because he isn't a member so I can't tell him shit, and he doesn't ask.

"And your woman's okay with this?"

"Haven't really gotten down to tell her."

He groans, "Damnit Logan, that shit got doomsday disaster all over it. Dad know?"

"He will, come sunset."

I hear the female voice in the background and I know his talk time is up.

"Don't worry about it, you'll be out before you know it."

He grumbles, "That's why I called asshole, not to listen to you dig your own grave. Doc is releasing me a week early. I'll be home soon, was thinking of coming to Kanla. Marcel is running the company for me. I need you to get me a place."

"Why don't you stay in the Clubhouse?"

"I'm not cleaning no toilets!" We both laugh as we say our goodbyes and I'm a whole lot better with his news.

It's not much time later that I hear Beggar come into the kitchen.

Her legs are making up the distance in a slow perusal toward me.

She's nervous.

I've never seen her nervous before. It's a first and shoot me if I'm not turned the hell on.

I'm standing by the oven making extra eggs for Aron and Venus but my eyes are trained on Beggar.

"You done with your family?" My question comes out casual but we both know it's not.

"Yes, he's my cousin, harmless if you family." She shrugs, like it's no big deal.

Beggar is clueless of how sexy she looks when she lifts her shoulder.

Her finger nails form an invisible trail as she steps closer to me.

Her jeans shape her ass, hinting at her curves.

I've never known a pair of baggy jeans could be so sexy on a woman until I saw Beggar in one. Her black eyes capture all my restraint. Draining me of logical sense at just one stare.

I drop the spatula, put the stove off.

My feet take up the remaining distance in four long strides.

I grab her ass and I'm tongue deep in her fucking throat.

Her tits rub my t-shirt covered chest as I grind my cock close to her heat. And I'm glad I took my cut off before cooking.

I love how tall she is.

I love how my cock rubs her abdomen. She's sensitive there.

I stop the kiss and place my forehead to hers, my breathing harsh,

"Tell me your name." I'm not sure why I ask it, I'm not certain why I even say what I say next either.

XXIII

"Tell me your name." He asks again.

It's on the tip of my tongue to say it. But I can't, the words won't come.

Instead I break out of his safety and say the only answer I can,

"Beggar, that's my name."

I don't look up. I can't bare it any more.

The disappointment etched on his beautifully scarred face will no doubt undo me.

"You keep lying to me Beauty. Fuck, how am I supposed to protect you, keep you safe?!" He hits the wall behind me and I jump from the impact.

"When I don't even know your name."

His eyes shine with disappointment and hurt, my heart splinting.

"I'm leaving, I'm being deployed and I don't know if I'm coming back, and I don't wanna die without even knowing your name. I don't wanna leave without knowing you safe, please I'm begging you."

His pleading with me makes it harder to refuse.

Why, why does he want the one thing I can't give him.

The one thing that will surely shatter his world.

Silent tears leak down my cheek, my throat clogging, it hurts, but nothing like my chest,

"I'm glad I got on the back of your bike that night Zero, and I'm even more glad that you spent the night in my bed. But you gotta let this go, you do protect me. When I'm in your arms I feel most protected, but spilling blood for me is not the answer. I can't tell you my name because I'm not her anymore, she wasn't someone I was proud of. She died a long time ago."

His face hardens, "I just want to know your name. Just one thing."

He pushes past me.

I want to stop him, run after him. My mind is screaming to me, telling me to go after him, tell him the truth.

But you know what they say, you tell so many lies that eventually they start becoming real.

All those lies become truths, until you don't know where the lie even started.

I'M DUSTING UP THE bar area, all the guys and girls have left apart from Killer, Aron and I.

I wanted to stayed behind with Aron to wait for Kylie Bray. It's my first time meeting the girl who got the VP wrapped around her pinky. Killer warned me she could be a trouble maker but I'm curious.

More so when I heard Vincent has a thing for her.

Aren't they related?

"Aron, get your behind downstairs now. We gotta make tracks." The loud twang accompanying the clapping heels coming from the front door perks me up. No greeting or pleasantries.

She walks in like she owns the place.

Her red snake skin heels are the first thing I see of hers as she turns the corner to where I am.

She startles when she spots me, but no unfamiliar surprise.

Someone must've told her about me. I take in her shiny, naked legs and the blue sundress she has on that stops by the top of her thighs.

Her long legs make up the small distance between us already extending her hand to me before she even gets here.

I wipe my own on the denim shorts Chadley said was part of the uniform when we had other Chapters around.

"The name's Kylie Bray sugar, you lookin' mighty fine in those cut offs." My mouth gaps at her bluntness.

The amused twinkle on her stunning face and slight smirk is not something I've seen on a girl before.

Which is why I'm standing here speechless.

She has this silent confidence that screams rich and privileged.

Why she's talking to me? I doubt she'll give me the time of day if she met me on the street begging for her scraps.

But she's Killers sister and Storm's girl, that's enough for me.

"Beggar. You want something to drink?"

I'm aware that Kylie is three years younger than me, so offering her alcohol is against the rules unless I'm told other-wise.

I'm also aware that I look at least five to six years older than her when I'm barely three.

"I can get it myself." She chirps but makes even that annoying sound, cool.

Kylie Bray is something else.

She tilts her head to the side the same way Aron likes to do. He's in Killer's room playing PlayStation with his uncle.

The thought makes me smile and has Kylie giving me speculative look,

"So, what's your story Beggar, besides the fact that you were a beggar and shacking up with my heartless jackass friend Zero, and don't deny it."

The all-knowing glance she gives me from across the bar while I dry the glasses makes me want to laugh.

She's so young and carefree, something I've never had a chance to be. *I like her*

"Not much to tell," I say as I put the dry glass on the tray in front of me and grab another.

"Or plenty to tell, and I just don't trust you Kylie, well not yet anyway." She answers back with an arch of her brow before standing up from the bar stool she was sitting on.

"Not much to tell, you already know I've lived on the streets my whole life. I'm 21 and shacking up is not the word for what Zero and I are doing. He sleeps in my bed."

"Right," She drags out.

Kylie is taller than me by a good couple inches. Her body is lean and toned, that would look just as nice encased in black jeans and a bright yellow vest with a catch phrase, 'Pleeeease let it knock you,' as the short blue number she's wearing.

Her make-up free face breaks into a big smile, "So, wanna join me for lunch Beggar, say 2 weeks' time?"

"You wanna have lunch with me?"

She looks affronted by whatever she sees on my face and loses some of that smile.

"Well I wouldn't ask if I didn't, sheesh woman," She snaps.

I think it over, as she mumbles something like, 'what's there to think about.'

I'm not a hundred percent certain I'll be here, but I nod with a small smile of my own.

"Great, I'll see myself out once Aron gets his ass in my car," She says this while pulling a soda pop from the fridge next to me.

"What should I tell Storm?" I ask.

Her response is a tinge of red marking her cheeks,

"Nothing he doesn't already know."

She winks at me with a salute before she walks off. I watch her go, shoulders back, feet sure and brisk.

Will I ever be able to do that? The thought is absurd and dumb, I'm never going to.

I skipped feminism the day I was born.

I'm just a beggar.

With that thought I get back to my job of clearing the bar. My first paying job.

I'm thankful to The Satan Snipers that I'm not sleeping on the streets and I'm a long way from Washington.

I would never allow the Famiglia to claim me. I couldn't.

I wouldn't force my family into a war. Which is why I can't let The Satan Snipers help me too.

My new start just has to wait another time.

The club hasn't made a decision on what they plan on doing.

Rounder told me that whatever they decide I'll be safe. What he doesn't know, is that as long as Lucca breathes, I will never be safe.

My day passes without a word from Zero and it's the first time I'm left alone in this big farm house.

I spend my day cleaning, vacuuming the carpets and wiping the floors. Anything to get my mind to quieten.

A setting sun and still no sign of anyone besides Killer who got a call and left hours ago.

I head up to my room.

Kylie and Aron are probably back in New York by now. She gave me her number to give her a call if I was ever in Washington again.

A few days ago, I would have laughed about that happening. No way was I setting foot in that place.

Now I'm laughing because ain't I the poster girl for shit luck.

I shake my head as I look at my leather bag ducking partially under the bed. I bend down, pick it up and throw it on top.

My night comes to show its haunting presence, reminding me of my limited time with Zero.

He hasn't called and I don't blame him.

He asked me for one thing, and it's a basic question to some, but I'm not just some.

A part of me wants to curl up in a ball and cry for hurting a man that I hardly know, but yet has come to mean so much to me it's confusing at the same time amazing.

A man that saves me a little each day.

Another part of me wants to curse him and hurt him for asking for the one thing I'll never be able to give him.

But the rest of me, the hardened pieces, the dead soul that is my making owns me.

Contrary to what the club thinks, I'm not a damsel in distress. I just have bad dreams and a monster that won't leave me alone.

I am a survivor.

The evidence is in the black leather zipped bag that sits on my bed in front of me.

I don't open it, not yet but soon.

It's hours later when the bikers get back.

I hear the rumbles just as I'm jumping into the bath tub of scalding water.

My head goes back to rest against the soft bath pillow. My eyes close as I relax.

"You look like a man's wet dream. Did you miss me Beauty?" I jump at the sound of his grunting voice, the water splashing on the floor and a bit on to Zero's shoes. Shiny shoes. Formal shoes.

My eyes do a slow and very thorough perusal of his body. He looks like my wet dream and it's no hardship when I say,

"Yes."

The black suit he has on is sculpted to his big frame. His thighs fill out the slacks as he steps closer to me and sits on the corner of the bath tub.

I want to ask him a million questions and demand a billion answers but instead I get up and let the water drip off my naked flesh as I sit on the tub mimicking his pose except my feet stay in the water.

"I missed you a lot." I'm sitting naked on the edge of the tub, perfectly entwined with his suit covered body.

"Then why are you sitting all the way over there, come show me how much you missed me."

My brass leaves me, as I slowly twist into him, my mouth closer to his lips, and kiss him, it's a peck, a test.

I can't believe he is here, in the bathroom, with such hunger in his eyes after everything. He grips my left hip, and it's a dirty reminder that my body is wet and naked against his hands, that are rough and big.

Trailing his fingers down my wet thigh, until he reaches the back of my knee, he slips his hand between my thighs, fast, until he cups my pussy. I gasp at the different feeling in his touch, I knew Zero is a man of action, but not like this.

Zero slips his hand and then arm under my pussy, until his arm is lodged in the crack of my ass, all the while looking at my face. His eyes burning me, as he lifts my body with his one arm.

Instinctively I wrap my legs around him, then he's kissing me. His mouth is angry, hungry, his hands rubbing my ass harshly, that it pains, but such a sexy kind of pain.

I hear his zipper in the back of my mind, then his cock is plunging into me. I scream, it burns, it's throbbing, his grip on my ass, the sting of his teeth in the crevice of my neck. This is too much.

He pounds into me, hard, my body jerking on him, my naked breast smacking his suit covered chest.

He lifts me up, his dick still hot and pulsing, as he carries me to the bathroom wall.

When my back hits the wall, I feel him deep in my womb as he plunges into me. He opens the door of the bathroom leading me to the bed that he flings me on. He grabs my legs, flipping me over.

My heart is thumping, my pussy throbbing, ass in the air, he rubs his dick around my pussy opening and plunges in.

He's not gentle, Zero is rough, and oh so lovely.

He's relentless, there's no sweet caresses, no tit groping, just hands on my hips, cold fucking.

This morning I told him I wanted to know what it is to be with him, I told him I wanted him to show me, show me why I shouldn't give him up.

He warned me that he'll consume me and I was too stubborn to listen. With each slap of his balls to my butt and each grunt he makes, I'm so glad I didn't.

The swell of his cock tightens my walls as he plants his seed right in my womb.

His eyes are half-mast when he takes his head out from the crook of my neck. It's then I feel the slight sting and a trickle.

"We didn't wrap."

"What?" He still has his sex voice, but there's something in it that is ringing warning bells, but I'm too sated to clear my head, so I reply,

"We didn't wrap."

His eyes lock on me, his jaw clenches, and just like the first time he over powered me, he does it again. My hands above my head, legs opened. The only difference is the cold metal digging into my wrist.

I'm on my back, naked on the bed, his cum dripping from between my legs that are splayed open.

"You think you so clever, Amariya Demarco, you thought I wouldn't find out. I was just a fucking means to an end, right? Did you enjoy yourself? Was messing with my mind, pretending to be some messed up broken damsel when really you nothing but a fucked-up bitch, a game to you?" My eyes widen at the mention of my name, and I struggle to get him off me.

His cold green eyes freeze me in place as his hand pulls on the small chain between the cuffs.

It's in these seconds that I know it's over. The feelings Zero has for me dies as I stare into his eyes.

The betrayal I see in them suffocates me, the disappointment that flashes in his gaze prepares me, and the anger, his anger just breaks me.

"My past is my past, I did what I had, to survive. I never claimed to be a damsel. Let me go and I'll leave."

He glares at me, pushing his suit covered body off me and slips on his pants.

I scramble up, until my back hits the headboard, my knees to my chest and my bound hands to my toes. I have no hair to cover me because it's tied to the top of my head.

Once his pants are on, Zero, slips a paper from his pocket and marches back to me. I don't need to look at the paper to know what it is.

I recite it.

"Name: Amariya Demarco

Age: unknown

Date of birth: Unknown

Father: Castelo Demarco

Mother: Mariete Demarco

Spouses: None

Girls last whereabouts? Deceased.

Causes: Unknown

Age of death: 16

Conclusion: Wanted for the murder of eleven victims. DNA was found at the scene of five crimes. Defendant is not deceased but now a Jane doe aka Beggar.

Wanted alive for 500000 cash. Contact Thorn Kade at A-List P.I."

Zero crumbles up the paper and flings it across the wall. His fingers grip my jaw and he snarls,

"So, I was just the fuck you to my brother? You tried to kill him, and then what? Got angry when he didn't die? Was almost getting Falon raped a set up."

His hold on my jaw tightens and I'm scared. My time with Lucca taught me that when a man has made up his mind, there's no words that will change it. And as I stare into the Enforcers eyes, I know he has made up his mind.

He is going to kill me.

The resolve in my eyes must be evident because he makes his first and only mistake. He leaves the room.

I spring into action with my hands cuffed. I grab my bag from under the bed unzip it and pull out the pliers.

After a bare minute I'm out of the hand cuffs. My jeans from the bag is next as I slide it up my legs.

My black tank top is slipped on next as I grab my leather hoody and my jacket.

I zip up the bag with my boots inside and go to the bedroom window.

The door bursts open and Knight and Storm charge in.

The darts from my leather jacket meet my fingers as they fly through the air getting both men.

Knight in his neck and Storm on his arm. Storm manages a few more steps before he falls.

Knight just drops.

I pull up the window as I grab my wall grippers from my bag. I attach them to my hands and climb out the window.

Zero's angry face is the last thing I see before I go down the wall.

My fall to the end is hard, and I twist my ankle but I know it's a matter of seconds before they open the door so I keep moving.

A few bikers come out, and I have no choice but to put darts in them.

I don't miss, I never miss.

I barely make it to the gate before Texas grabs me from around the waist and throws me hard against the ground.

The dart in my hand goes into his stomach.

His hands wrap around my throat, sucking off my oxygen supply. I wheeze, pulling at his arms.

It's a sufferable minute before he's out. I only gave them a tranquilizer that will last for four hours. Deno slipped them into my bag.

My phone chimes letting me know my ride is here.

I was hoping to leave quietly. Not like this.

My vision goes to the bedroom window and I see the man that will always own the last shred of my humanity.

I see the man that will always own the pieces of me. My back turns to him because I know that my story with Zero has ended.

He will never forgive me, just like how I can never be sorry.

I will kill his brother if I got the chance.

I will finish what I started.

The gates open as the mass of Mercedes stop.

Lucca and his men all pull out their guns stopping the bikers from coming any closer to me and for the first and only time I actually seek shelter from my monster.

I walk closer to Lucca, each step a journey closer to hell.

His hazel eyes stay focus on the bikers until I am in touching distance.

I watch as he signals his men. Jade and Falon run from the back. Jade hitting my shoulder.

I look up into my monster's eyes.

"Lucca," I say as I die a thousand deaths.

He smiles and it's so cold, that I'm scared even hell would freeze if it looked into his soul.

"Welcome back wife."

Thank you Reading my book

Please take a minute to leave a review or send me an email to let me know what you thought about Zero and Beggar's story. Their story continues in Zero but before you jump on The Satan Sniper's wagon again, please enjoy the small piece of Kylie Bray's story.

I have written 3 series that are all linked together in different places, but will all be joined as the series all progress and the entire plot develops.

While you may read all the series separately without missing anything, to really enjoy this world I have created from a simple thought, I suggest you read all the books.

For any further questions or suggestions or if you need a friend and want to say hi, email me on shanrk@zoho.com

Don't miss out!

Visit the website below and you can sign up to receive emails whenever Shan R.K publishes a new book. There's no charge and no obligation.

https://books2read.com/r/B-A-DHHG-JBDT

BOOKS 2 READ

Connecting independent readers to independent writers.

Did you love *Beggar*? Then you should read *Kylie Bray*[1] by Shan R.K!

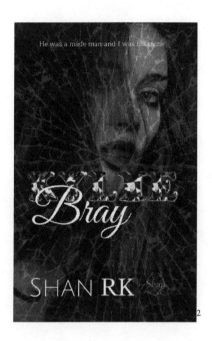

A Mafia Novel About Love, Hate And Billions.

I had two great loves.

The first had the power to weaken me.

The second broke me.

Vincent Stone was my addiction before he turned out to be my disease

Our love was forbidden, he was my stepbrother

But that wasn't the worst of it all

No, you see, he was a Made Man and I was his Muse

---

1. https://books2read.com/u/bMQPvk

2. https://books2read.com/u/bMQPvk

A full length Standalone novel about an Heiress and a Savage Killer.

For mature audience only.

Read more at https://shanrk.com.

Also by Shan R.K

Catch Me, If You Can
Shock Me Twice

Liston Hills
School Me Season 1
School Me Season 2
School Me Season 3

Love Hate and Billions
Kylie Bray

Secrets Of The Famiglia
Capo Dei Capi

The Angel Descendants
House Of Legions

The Satan Sniper's Motorcycle Club
Beggar
River's Keeper
Zero
Beauty's Breath

Standalone
Faces Of You

Watch for more at https://shanrk.com.

About the Author

I am a born and bred South African Author.

My passion for writing was not something that suddenly happened. I was born to write words as one is born to die.

My stories are dark and twisted. The Characters are people who we all can relate to.

They are either personas of a certain belief of mine or they are characters portraying the different types of people in our world today.

I love writing fiction and bringing a world alive with words. I believe that a voice is not just one spoken but one seen too.

Since I have started writing I am able to show you that which I wish to scream.

I enjoy reading at any time of day.

My favourite book I have read to date would be Angels blood by **Nilini Singh**. My ATF Author is a definite **Jamie Begley** and my BR series is split between Infernal Devices by

Cassandra Clare and The Black daggerhood brothers by **J.R Ward**.

The longest book I have written to date would go to House of Legions- A paranormal romance about a Lightwatcher and Angel.

The best book I have written would be Beggar - A MC suspense/romance series.

The best idea I have ever had would be to start my blog Liston Hills School me. It is a live online novel I started working on a year ago.

If I could describe myself I would say I am shy but also friendly.

Read more at https://shanrk.com.

Made in the USA
Monee, IL
30 October 2024